Deceit in Dixie

by

Kim Chosie

Down South, Book 2

Cover Art by *Tina Lynn Stout*

The Wild Rose Press, Inc.
PO Box 708
Adams Basin, NY 14410-0708
Visit us at www.thewildrosepress.com

Publishing History
First Edition, 2024
Trade Paperback ISBN 978-1-5092-5455-2
Digital ISBN 978-1-5092-5456-9

Down South, Book 2
Published in the United States of America

Dedication

To my people: My Sexy Man, Carmen, Elligrace and Libby.

Chapter 1

Zoey materialized in the kitchen earlier than usual wearing an oversized FSU jersey, red fleece sweatpants, and sporting a ponytail on the top of her head. She had pronounced sheet marks across her face and sleepy eyes with a little crust in the corners. Her famous morning look. At fifteen she was a fashion conscious, studious young lady and an overgrown child who still played with Legos and watched Sponge Bob. She plopped onto the stool next to the kitchen bar and I handed her a cup of coffee.

"Rough night?" I asked.

"Usual," she said, taking the cup and adding a squirt of Hershey's syrup from the squeeze bottle I set out for her. She took a sip of her chocolate coffee and grabbed a Cannoli from the plate on the counter. "I wish we had a Veniero's bakery here," she lamented. These were a present from Lisa's last trip to NYC I had stashed in the freezer so they would last more than a day.

"What was usual?" Mase asked as he rushed through the kitchen reaching for a cup of coffee and stuffing a Cannoli into his mouth. He was dressed in workout attire (sans the Cannoli) and heading for the gym.

"Oh you know," Z said, "The usual drunken stupidity. The random hook-ups, the drama. I'm really tired of the whole scene." She took another sip from her coffee and the last bite of her cream filled treat. "It's time for a girl's trip, Mom. Let's make it happen." With that she topped off her cup and retreated into the living room to watch cartoons—a habit she had never outgrown.

"Gotta go, love." Mase grabbed his keys and puckered for a kiss. "Don't forget about dinner tonight with my parents and their parents," (he always referred to his grandparents that way) he said on his way out. "I'll try to make it short, but you know I love my parents' parents…they're not getting any younger."

"We'll be ready," I said, not dreading spending time with Olivia and Wes as much as I normally would because Gramps (Major) and Mimi (Ginny) would be there. They didn't much like Mase's mother Olivia, for reasons still not very clear, and they didn't do much to disguise it.

"Don't forget dinner at the club tonight," I reminded Zoey as I strolled with my morning caffeine outside onto the front porch.

"Geez, Mom, I hate that place." Silence. "Can I at least bring RJ?"

"Sure. Whatever makes it bearable."

I perched on the cushioned porch swing and gently glided back and forth in the early morning freshness. This truly was the best part of the year. Fall. The weather cooled to a more tolerable degree and the humidity was almost nonexistent until early afternoon. Fragrant marigolds liberated the distinct scent of licorice into the air. And the piece de resistance, a newly redesigned porch for a magazine photo shoot because my house was "vintage", which I thought just meant old until a former Banjoland freelancer remembered it and wanted to use it for a segment of retro outdoor displays in the next summer issue of *Southern Life*. The only thing that could make it better was for us to have a baby. Mase and I began trying right after we were married, and that was eight years ago. The doctors said they didn't see a reason why we couldn't get pregnant, as tests revealed nothing physically wrong with either of us.

"Lanie, honey, it's okay," Mase had said after our last in what felt like weekly discussions on the topic. "If we have a baby, great, if not, we have Zoey and that's enough."

He was always so kind, but I knew deep down he wanted his own child. I could tell by the way his eyes lit up when we talked about in the early days.

Leese interrupted my thoughts when she skidded into my driveway on two wheels in her Audi sports coupe, dust from the road flying everywhere—a far cry from the truck with a gun rack she had been driving when she picked us up at the airport on our first day in Banjoland.

"Times have changed," she said, laughing when I commented on that difference.

AJ popped out of the passenger side first. At almost eight years old, he was taller than most his age, lanky, with dark brown shaggy hair and sparkly green eyes just like Lisa's. He was so filled with life it was hard to believe we almost lost him before he was born.

"Hey, Aunt Mel," he said, the only one who called me Mel besides Leese.

"Hey, buddy," I said. "Zoey's inside watching T.V."

"Cool." He breezed by me, flinging open the door to announce his entrance.

"Hey, why aren't you dressed?" Lisa asked, posing and modeling her new workout attire—she always had the latest. It was an addiction for her. It was our routine to do a killer cardio class on Saturday mornings while Adam and Mase did some bootcamp/CrossFit thing.

"Nice," I said. She had a fabulous body and regained her fitness quickly once she finished post-accident rehab. She tossed me the red and white distinctive bag. "Don't be jealous. I bought you something, too."

"Thanks! But sit for a minute. We have some time, and oh by the way, Mase and I have to meet the parents and grandparents for dinner tonight."

She took a sip from my coffee cup on the side table. "That's interesting."

It was more than interesting. I hadn't had a conversation with Olivia since we literally fought it out in her bedroom the night I found and repossessed the ledger almost a decade ago, not that I would say that was a legitimate chat. She had been out of the country residing in Andorra to avoid possible prosecution for Sunglasses murder since Senator Downes was convicted of bribery and extortion, and we didn't see or hear from her during this time.

Her attorney said she would probably not be convicted given the circumstances, but she did not want to take any chances of the senator using her situation with Sunglasses to coerce Mase into becoming one of his yes men. As far as we knew, no one else except the senator knew of her "situation" as we began to call it and whenever anyone asked about her, we simply said she was "off continent."

She returned just prior to his release from prison, and since she possessed the social grace of any prominent Southern bred woman, Mase predicted that after everything, she would pretend that our altercation and the recording from Andorra never happened. It was very strange to me, but Mase explained that ignoring the incident as if it never happened was her way of coping while still being able to acknowledge me.

These rules of engagement were too complicated for me to learn immediately, and it had taken time for me to become familiar with the specific protocols for each social situation. Fortunately, I had some help interpreting these rules and in eliminating the possibility of a faux pas at every social interaction.

"So how are you going to play it?" Leese asked, commandeering my coffee once and for all.

"Well, I'll just let Mimi take the lead, lay low, not say too much. You know she is going to say exactly what she thinks anyway—there comes an age where the rules of society don't apply—and it usually involves some way that Olivia has disappointed her over the years. Truthfully, it kinds of makes me feel a little badly for Olivia of the Atlanta Westhovens." I reclaimed my empty cup and Leese followed me into the kitchen. "I'm not even sure why she wants to play the happy family. I guess we'll just have to wait and see."

"I'd love to be a fly on her martini," Leese said.

It had been good to see New York Lisa reappear since Ad had become a senator. She did an excellent job living the dichotomy between Banjoland and the real world, as I still referred to our lives in SoHo. After the accident and the ensuing rehab, AJ's early years and Ad's seemingly never-ending political campaigning, she had found her niche.

"So what did we miss?" Lisa asked, referring to the liberation of the senator from a Federal work camp while they were out of town.

"Absolutely nothing," I said, "it was exactly how we

thought it would be except Olivia's parents were there— like it was a family reunion. Weird. They were in the background, discreet and unobtrusive, and I think because they were out of the chaos, no one really noticed them."

Lisa raised an eyebrow and motioned for me to pass a cannoli.

"Probably because they're a hundred years old," she said, taking a small bite of the pastry.

****

The news media were everywhere, just like when they covered his trial. I thought some of the reporters were even the same, or maybe they were just caricatures that all looked alike. They were pushing microphones in our faces, pleading for a comment. It was a circus, and I resented having to be there.

"Ready?" Mase asked, taking my hand and leading me toward the steps of the county jail where Senator Downes was transferred and where he would be officially released, and where Olivia was already in position, having returned from her self-imposed exile.

"Not really," I said, scoping the scene for an easy exit through the maze of satellite TV trucks and wannabe reporters.

"We can do this. We'll only stay until he gets into his limo and then we're out of here."

I knew we had to do it. Olivia made a point of explaining that we needed to show a united front, that no matter what happened we were family and needed to present a certain image to the public. There was no mention of our physical melee all those years ago, and without that acknowledgment it was almost like it never happened.

Something was different about her today. Her arrogant, condescending, bitchy attitude seemed more subdued than it had been right before he was sentenced, when the senator was certain he would be acquitted. That was a long time ago and before she left the country for the second time.

For this event she seemed more concerned that we appear as a family united. That somehow everyone would forget that the senator was a convicted felon, and that Olivia herself had killed a man.

She was certainly dressed to make an impression in her Carolina Herrera floral print and Jimmy Choo Crisscross sandals. As always, she appeared as the dutiful, long-suffering wife. It was a curious spectacle. We assumed our positions and on cue with cameras rolling, the jailhouse doors slowly opened.) Mason Westhoven Downes III emerged from his captivity in a crisp and fashionable Armani suit. Contrary to what I thought prison might do to someone, he looked healthy and fit, well groomed, and was smiling and waving to the cameras like he was part of the who's who on the red carpet. There was no humbleness, no sign of remorse. In fact, it looked like he was running for office again. He shook hands and chatted with some of his many supporters as he made his way over to us, occasionally leaning into whisper something to one of his constituents.

"Hello, honey," he said as he bent down and kissed Olivia on the cheek.

She smiled and retouched her foundation.

"Son," he said, acknowledging Mase, shaking his hand and leaning in for a hug. The media waited with anticipation for his response.

Mason stood stiffly and nodded but didn't speak or reciprocate. They would surely write something about that.

"You're as beautiful as ever, Lanie honey. I want to officially welcome you to our family in-person, albeit a little late." He kissed me on each cheek, like we were European, smiled briefly and turned to face the cameras. He was still quite handsome, his tall, broad, and solid manly frame evident as he walked up the steps while he spoke, making eye contact with each person along the way. He held up his hand to quiet the crowd. "I sincerely want to thank each one of you for your support during this unfortunate time..."

"Can we leave now?" I whispered to Mase.

He didn't answer, just pulled me by my hand behind the TV trucks, through support staff and over large black cords, cables, and wires, into the parking lot where he proceeded to open a beer from the cooler in the back of his truck.

"Can you believe that?" he asked, taking a long swig.

I most definitely could. "It was quite a spectacle."

Mase finished the rest of his beer, threw the can into the empty bucket in the truck bed, and opened another one for the road. I drove.

We were silent for a few miles until he spoke again.

"You know it's not over," he said, "he's had plenty of time to plan his return and he won't let Adam off the hook."

"I know."

Chapter 2

Olivia's parents, Tazewell "Major" Westhoven and Virginia Clements Westhoven, of the Atlanta Westhovens, were considered Southern Royalty, not only in the state of Georgia but also throughout the South.

Major's father, Colonel Ashley Lee Westhoven, was instrumental in helping the South win the battle of Chancellorsville during the Civil War. According to Olivia, and corroborated by historians, Colonel Westhoven fought directly under General Robert E. Lee and was responsible for stepping into the place of General Stonewall Jackson after he was killed by friendly fire. It was his decision to split the greatly outnumbered Southern Army and attack the Union Army, we had been repeatedly informed, a battle that went down in history as General Lee's perfect battle. Because of his role in this monumental victory, Colonel Westhoven returned home a hero.

Postwar, he was integral in developing the First National Bank of Atlanta and was President for decades before serving as Chairman of the Board—a position he held until he died, after which Major assumed it without a single dissenting vote from the board of directors.

What no one *ever* mentioned, except us, is that Olivia's father and Mase's father, Wes, were first cousins. Senator Downes' great grandmother and

Olivia's great grandfather were brother and sister. When I first became aware of this, I was shocked. I always thought it was illegal and incestuous to marry your cousin, but maybe not in the South? Mase acted like it was no big deal.

"If it's no big deal," I said, "why can't we speak of it?"

"Because some people won't understand," he said simply.

Lisa and I enjoyed this tidbit of information, though, and every time someone in Mase's family—or Mase—did something odd or unusual, our response was a covert smile and the comment "cousins", usually made under our breath in conjunction with a faux cough.

In the middle of my play by play for Lisa, the front door flew open and Zoey flew past me, purse and phone in hand.

"Bye, Mom, be home by midnight." She kissed my cheek and hurriedly slipped on her leather jacket and matching boots, gifts from Leese for her last birthday. "Hey, Leese," she added, giving her a quick peck on the cheek. She had dropped "aunt" a few months ago. Lisa didn't care.

"Where are you going?" I asked, not sure I remembered having this conversation.

"RJ got off work early, so he and Greggins are coming by and we're going to go help his mom fix the fence gate, eat supper and then to Mac Brown's field party, remember?"

RJ's truck pulled slowly into the drive—speed had been a topic of several conversations—she pecked me once more, said bye to Leese and was gone, long red humidity curls and raspy voice trailing behind her.

"I wish he would come to the door for her," I observed.

"No worries," Leese said. "He's come a long way. And she's a good girl."

All of that was true.

RJ had come such a long way since Ray was killed in the explosion at the Wine and Swine festival when he was a boy. He and Zoey were such different people. She had the advantage of being culturally sophisticated and traveled, in a non-snobby way, with a warm and genuine personality. He was kind, hardworking, also cultured, but in the Banjoland ways. The first time he came with us on a trip to New York I thought he might be permanently scarred. Lisa and I, and Zoey, thought incorporating a few traditional stops for a first-time visitor would make our quarterly shopping trip more bearable for him, so we added visits to the Statue of Liberty and Central Park, which he handled well—like a Japanese tourist. Oohing and ahhing, posing for random Instagram pics with Z for proof that he had, in fact, traveled to this foreign land.

He couldn't make sense of anything outside of the historical sites. He didn't understand why people could not carry a concealed weapon, why everyone was in such a hurry all the time, why there seemed to be such an overabundance of concrete and people and taxicabs. Everybody he spoke to was enthralled with his accent and would ask him to repeat himself just so they could hear his drawl one more time. It was like he was some rare creature that they would never get the opportunity to see again—like bigfoot, a once in a lifetime opportunity. He didn't respond well to being on display, but endured it with his Southern, gentlemanly charm. What he did love, and initially try to hide, was his fondness for musical theater. I discovered this juicy morsel when I told him the first show we were going to see while we were in the City was *Les Miserables*.

"It's based on a novel by Victor Hugo," Leese explained, "about the redemption of a man named Jean Valjean."

RJ was standing in front of the mirror adjusting his tie, and responded casually while tightening the knot, "He judged society and condemned it."

We were stunned. Well, not Zoey. She beamed at him. He was smiling proudly.

"It's one of my favorites," he added.

****

I toweled off after an extra-long hot shower pondering this journey of my life and began my preparations for dinner at the Club.

"Hey, baby," he whispered. "Miss me?" He grabbed me from behind and ghosted my neck with his lips—the start of his traditional foreplay.

I smiled instinctively and pushed back the hope that maybe this time would be *the* time. The anxiety of wondering if we would ever have our own child and wondering if we should give up trying entered my mind every time we had sex now, but as always, I did my best to let myself relax and become distracted by his smell and the feel of his touch. Just as things were heating up, I heard Queen singing, *"You're my Best Friend,"* from my cell that was on the nightstand. It was Lisa's ringtone, and Mase and I had an understanding ever since the accident that I would always take her calls no matter what time it was or what we were doing. He was usually tolerant.

"Hey," I said, trying to catch my breath, "everything OK?"

"Oh, God, I interrupted you two again, didn't I?"

"No worries," I said. "What's up?"

"Tell her that her timing is exceptional, as always," Mase said, as he climbed into the shower.

"I heard," she said, "but if you weren't always doing it there might be a chance I could call and not be a third party in your love sessions."

We both laughed at "love sessions."

"Anyway, the reason I'm calling is because Ad just came in after meeting with some local donors, and word is that Olivia's parents are in town because her father is handing over the chairmanship of the bank to Senator Downes."

"Interesting," I said. "I'll call you tomorrow and let you know what I find out."

"Please, do, and Lane, remember, listen to what Mimi says. . . and what she doesn't say."

It had been calm while the senator was in prison, relatively, for Banjoland. Everyone went about their business as usual and no one spoke of the future explicitly or specifically, as it pertained to the senator himself. I had a feeling all of that was about to change.

Chapter 3

We arrived at the club running late and sped into the parking lot, bypassing the usual stop to show identification formality. Jonah recognized each one of our vehicles, so all we had to do was give him the cursory wave or smile and we cruised right in.

We'd had the conversation prep on the ride over. Topics acceptable for conversation: the weather, school, Z's upcoming sixteenth birthday, anything related to hunting or new accessories/bows/guns and football—college preferably, high school acceptable. Some free-style discussion was allowed if topics were generic. A nod by Mase or myself was required to proceed. Topics off limits: the senator's incarceration, Olivia's jet setting, the senator's future plans, rumors of Olivia's indiscretions while he was incarcerated, her future plans, Ad and/or Lisa, AJ, and anything else deemed too controversial, once again decided by a glance from Mase or me.

We piled out of Mase's truck, all dreading the command appearance, but we did make a good-looking family, plus one. RJ was a good sport, considering we spent fifteen minutes explaining why he couldn't wear his camo attire. He knew the dress code—it's not like he hadn't been there before with us—but nevertheless I think he felt like he had to try.

"I just don't see why they can't accept me how I

am," he would say.

"They don't accept anybody how they are," I would reply. It was the same conversation every time. I think he just felt like he owed it to himself to have the dialogue.

Mase parked in front of the entrance and tossed his keys to Greggins, as he recently began parking cars at the Club.

"Hey, all," he said, smiling pleasantly. "Been waiting to get my hands behind the wheel of this baby," referring to Mase's new Ford pickup.

Greg was a typical young man for the area. He was a jack of all trades, and to make money he did mechanic work on people's vehicles, did some home repair work, and most recently had become a type of errand boy for Senator Downes. He would make deliveries, pick up money or documents, or even chauffeur Olivia from one place to another. He spent most of his out of school hours working in some way.

We first met him not long after Mase and I became a couple. He appeared to be a few years younger than Zoey and proudly introduced himself to us one Saturday when we stopped by the Downes' to drop off some mail accidentally sent to Mase instead of the senator (happened often). His mother was their housekeeper and his father, we were told later, was out of the picture.

"Hi." He flung the door open as we approached.

"What's your name?" Zoey piped up, pushing between us to get a better look at this pint-sized freckled pixie with the flaming red mane.

"Greggins McCain McGreggor," he said proudly, holding out his hand as he'd obviously been taught. He was the housekeeper's son.

No slacker in the manners department herself, Z

held out her hand and replied, "My name is Zoey, but you can call me Z."

"Come with me, Z." He motioned for her to follow. She ran behind him through the kitchen, red manes disappearing out the back door. They could have been siblings.

****

"Hey, Simon," we said in unison as we went through the open door.

"Hey, Downes family plus one," he said. "They are already a few drinks in." He nodded toward the cluster of folks gathered under the elephantine chandelier in the center of the room.

Well, that was just adding fuel to the fire, in my opinion, but I wasn't worried one bit. Tonight I was a bystander, simply there as a prop for whatever performance was on display. We smiled as Simon held the door until we all passed through, making our way as we had so many times before, to the family table. There were only a few families that had their own tables, as they were reserved for the legacies of club founders or significant donors.

The always predictable minions, flitting around like gnats, shifted slightly to make room for us as we neared the table, but those that had not yet paid their respects to the faux royalty jockeyed for position. Amid the "Senator, glad to see you!" and "Trumped up charges!" and "Over here, sir!" shouts and hollers, the grandmaster rose from his seat at the table, whiskey glass in one hand, Cuban in the other, always the campaigner.

"Thanks, everyone." He exhaled cigar smoke and toasted the crowd. "It's good to be back where I belong." There were a few cheers and some light clapping. "But

16

as I'm sure you can understand, I'd like to spend some time getting reacquainted with my family, so if you don't mind allowing us to have dinner, I'll be glad to talk with all of you when we're finished." With that the regular people dispersed, leaving only us and the small army of wait staff lingering close by.

"Sit, sit," the senator said to everyone, pulling out my chair while RJ got Zoey's.

After some awkward small talk and quickly filled drink orders, Olivia, still sporting her summer tan, excused herself abruptly and made her way to the bar, slipping onto a stool between an older, thin gentleman with gray hair and thick sideburns that matched his sport coat and a young guy with curly brown locks wearing a short sleeve polo that revealed his chiseled arms. No one seemed to think this was in any way odd except Mase and me. Senator Downes was still chatting with his dad, apparently unfazed, and Z and RJ were both texting under the table. We shot each other a quizzical look as the senator tapped the side of his glass with a butter knife.

"I'm sure you are wondering why I had Olivia ask you all to be here tonight," he said in his smooth baritone voice.

I elbowed Zoey to pay attention and she immediately looked up from her phone. She did the same to RJ.

"Dad, why don't you make it official?" He turned toward Major, who looked like he was almost asleep.

Major reminded me of a tree trunk, solid and thick, but clearly age had weathered his branches. His face looked like a piece of shriveled fruit, though it was obvious that he had been handsome once, and he still had dimples and a smile that were surprisingly captivating.

He struggled to stand and held himself steady with one hand on the table. Clearing his throat and speaking distinctly, he said, "I'm sure you've all realized that I'm getting a tad older." The dying swan. We smiled politely in return. "And so now I think it's time to turn over my long-held position as Chairman of First National. I can't think of a better successor than my son, our own Wes Downes." He held up his wine glass with his free hand. "Here's to Wes and to a new era at First Fed."

Senator Downes was literally beaming. We all held up our glasses.

"Here's to Wes/Dad/Senator Downes," we said in unison.

"To my son," Mimi interjected in her gravelly Southern drawl. She had been unusually quiet all night, and with everything else going on, I had almost forgotten she was there.

This news itself wasn't surprising to me, as Mase and I had the heads up from Leese. There had also been rumors. What did confuse me was the how and why this could happen. Can a convicted felon be the chairman of a bank? What did he even know about the banking industry? Turns out he could, especially if his family founded the bank. While I was pondering these and other questions, my cell phone vibrated unexpectedly. I slipped it out of my clutch nonchalantly, glad I had remembered to turn off the sound. It was a text from Leese.

"Look up," it said.

I did. There they were. Ad, Leese and AJ, along with some of the staff from Ad's office and his advisor in tow. I tossed my phone and smiled widely. She hadn't mentioned they were going to be here. She smiled and rolled her eyes in the "I know this could be very awkward, but I don't care and I'm glad you're here too," kind of way, kissed me on the cheek and followed a waiter to a table near the heavily draped windows, where three gentlemen in suits were already seated. Ad did the same.

Adam had no contact whatsoever with Senator Downes after he went to prison, understandably. Prison was more of a work camp where politicians and white-collar criminals spent their days doing little more than watching TV, with the exception of those that took advantage of the state-of-the art fitness center, library and networking opportunities. When Ad ran for Congress, he had to address his relationship with Senator Downes quite a bit at first. His campaign machine did an excellent job of distancing itself from the senator and his dealings, walking the line between portraying Ad as ignorant of the senator's illegal activities, but not making him appear naïve or incapable. This was the first time they had been in the same room together since the trial.

Worlds were about to collide.

Senator Downes thanked us for our support, glanced at the bar at Olivia who had become cemented on her stool and engaged in conversation with the hot guy and a few of his posse, and pushed himself away from the table. For a moment I thought he was going to get her. I was wrong.

He brushed some rogue ashes from his trousers, straightened his tie, and proceeded boldly with his trademark stride toward Ad's table. As I watched the scene unfold in seeming slow motion, strains from *The Godfather* began their crescendo from the musical recesses in my mind. Senator Downes, his 6 feet 4-inch meaty frame larger than life, reached Adam's table in 4 strides. Lisa dropped the fork full of salad she was about to inhale and stared at him like she was paralyzed. At any moment I expected Mafioso hit men to burst into the dining room and methodically begin taking us out one by one.

Mental Note: I need to include this scene in my novel.

Everyone at Adam's table stopped eating and stared; obviously no one was sure what to expect. Except the suits. They were oblivious. Adam the politician was composed and confident. Mase and I were transfixed, voyeurs caught up in the anticipation.

Ad stood up as soon as he saw what was happening. It was the consummate performance, I must say. They hugged in the way that men do, shook hands, and appeared more like friends that hadn't seen each other in months than an ex-con and the guy he thought would be his patsy.

After a brief minute or two of whispered words and another hand on each other's shoulder for a moment, Ad sat back down, and the senator made his way over to the bar and whispered into Olivia's ear. She got up without responding to him and they left. The show was over for now.

Chapter 4

Fall was in full swing in Banjoland. The marching band was in formation blaring from the center of the field as we took our seats on the top row of the worn and splintered bleachers. The stadium was packed for this game, the final of the season against rival Butler County. It was the start of one of the biggest weekends of the fall. Tonight, local high school football. Saturday, rival college football between Florida State and Florida, and Sunday, opening day of dove hunting season—and in our world, Zoey's 16th birthday bash. It was an exciting time and tonight it began with RJ. He'd already been offered a football scholarship to State, and he'd led the Cougars to an undefeated season so far—their first in 20 years. The autumn air was crisp and the atmosphere electric, people smiling and socializing and in very high spirits. Mary Sue was exuberant—there was no sign of the unspoken sadness she'd been wearing like a blanket since Ray died. Tonight, she was overflowing with pride and absorbing all the congratulations like little happiness injections.

Zoey, Leese and I took our seats, glad to have remembered our Bullet Bobs seat cushions, behind Mary Sue, Billy Joe and Sue Ellen. Ad and Mase were supposed to join us after a meeting with the suits about the finances for Ad's upcoming campaign. I thought they'd be here by now. The pregame show was beginning.

"And now, ladies and gentlemen," a bass voice announced from the press box, "this year's most valuable player...starting quarterback number 14... Raymond...Jenkins...Junior!"

The crowd erupted. Everyone stood on their feet, clapping and cheering. Obviously basking in his moment, RJ followed the rest of the team to the sideline down below, jumping up and down, waving to the crowd and nodding and pointing at us. Ray certainly would've been proud. Since RJ's first attempt at tackling a greasy pig when he was 5 years old at the Wine and Swine festival, he had been on a predetermined path guided by memories of Ray.

Greggins, who took advantage of most any opportunity to make money, was selling popcorn and hotdogs a few rows down.

"Look." Leese jabbed her elbow into my arm and motioned for me to follow her gaze.

"What?" It was dusk and difficult to see. I squinted but could barely make out the silhouettes of two figures talking near what looked like a sports car at the entrance to the parking lot.

"Here." She handed me a small pair of high-powered binoculars she pulled from her purse. The fact that she always had binoculars in her purse stemmed from her post accident need to see (paranoia we all thought) who was approaching far in advance and had now turned into a practical tool with a variety of uses. It didn't even seem odd anymore.

I put the field glasses to my eyes and adjusted the knobs until a clear image of Olivia appeared sitting behind the steering wheel of her sleek black Mercedes

Coupe. An exotic looking woman holding the hand of a small child was talking to her intently through the window. After a few minutes Olivia handed her what looked like a small envelope and the woman leaned through the window and kissed Olivia's cheek, turned and walked away, the young boy with her trailing close behind. It was odd that Olivia was here at the school, because it was just a place she didn't fit. Maybe she arranged to meet this woman here because everyone else in town was here tonight for the big game.

I lowered the glasses and handed them back to Leese without comment.

****

I woke up the next morning with cottonmouth, bedhead and half dressed. It took me a minute to orient myself. I was relieved to find Mase next to me under the covers, naked. I scrounged around for my panties and jeans and quietly dressed before I crept down the hall and into the kitchen, surprised to see Ad already up and making coffee.

"And how are we feeling this morning, Lanie Lou?" he asked, sounding chipper.

I gave him my famous pre-coffee death stare and didn't answer. I sat at the bar, rested my head on the cool granite surface and closed my eyes. My head throbbed.

About that time, I heard a door creak open and some shuffling from the hallway. I cracked open my eyes to see Lisa standing in the doorway, make-up from last night smeared under her bloodshot green eyes, hair knotted in the ponytail she slept in, and wearing what could only be described as cartoon couture; a Betty Boop t-shirt, plaid boxers and Flintstone socks with Fred, Wilma and Pebbles on one, and Barney, Betty and Bam

23

Bam on the other.

I closed my eyes again and she fell onto the stool next to me and assumed the same position.

After the Cougars trounced Butler County, the celebration lasted into the early morning hours. We, the responsible parents, gave Zoey and RJ a curfew of 1:00 a.m., since it was a special occasion, while we sat on the porch at Lisa's, drinking shots and talking about the time Ad had to bail us out of jail because we'd had too much to drink at the annual Saint Patrick's day parade and got a little zealous at the Flannigans' after-party and started riding the Shriner's little scooters through the upper West Side. Ad retold the story in great detail while Mase egged him on. We talked about his upcoming re-election campaign, Zoey's birthday, college, and before we knew it, the night had passed into morning. It was fun and relaxing, and I didn't mention anything to Mase about seeing Olivia at the game. It might have been nothing, but I had a weird feeling it might be something, so I decided to just sit on the sighting until there was a reason to mention it. The guys went to bed after Z called from home because we had decided when the shots began, we would be spending the night at Lisa's house, and honestly the guys just couldn't hang with us when we were on a drinking roll. I made Z Facetime us in front of the kitchen clock so I knew she was home when she said she was there—knowing fully she could leave again—and going through the motions, because I knew she was trustworthy, but also because it fulfilled part of my parental responsibility. I had no reason to doubt her and I didn't really, but it doesn't hurt to verify occasionally. Leese and I were now drunk and alone, which allowed for more blunt conversation than when our men were around.

"What do you think is up with Olivia?" she blurted, referring to Olivia's recent request that Mase and I meet her at the club for lunch. I thought our recent evening together gave us attendance credit for another year or so and I hoped this didn't mean we were starting a pattern of more frequent contact.

"No idea," I said honestly. "I was hoping our last interaction, as brief as it was, would be the last. . . at least for a while."

"Can you believe Z is sixteen?" she said, abruptly changing gears. She did that when she was drunk.

"No," I said. "She's been asking a few more questions about Junior lately," I added and took a long drink from my limey beer.

Zoey had very few real memories of Junior because she was so young when he died the first time, and she never asked many questions about him, except for the brief time when she was eight years old and one of her classmates called her real father a rapist. I don't think either of them knew what that really meant, but she knew it wasn't good and that was enough to really upset her.

"What are you telling her?" she asked, licking the leftover salt from the rim of her empty Margarita glass.

"Just that he wasn't a very nice guy, but that he loved her, yadda yadda. I still haven't told her that Mase shot him and why," I said. "I guess I'm going to have to do it sooner or later."

I thought about that for a minute.

"What do I say? Oh, by the way, I shot your dad when you were a baby because he was beating the crap out of me. I thought he was dead. Years later he showed up here and Mase shot him again when he tried to rape me. This time he really is dead. We're sure."

"Jesus, Mel, I wouldn't say it like that." She laughed half-heartedly. "You know, that book you're writing should really be about your life."

"I need to go to bed," I said, tiring of the subject and tossing my bottle into the large blue county recycling bin.

We stood up together and stumbled toward the door. Lisa fumbled with the handle but couldn't open it, and the ridiculous state of our drunkenness overcame me, causing me to start laughing uncontrollably. She looked at me for a moment as if wondering what was so funny until she too began laughing in that unreserved guttural laugh people do when they are completely uninhibited.

I reached for the door handle with one hand and held my finger up to her lips with the other, trying to shush her, but she pushed my hand away and pulled me around to face her. Without warning her soft lips touched mine and I tripped backwards and fell onto the old park bench she had situated next to the door.

I had been a very long time since Lisa kissed me. We'd only had one previous physical encounter and it was during one of the darkest times of my life. It was after a particularly brutal encounter with Junior that left me with a cracked rib and a tear in my cheek where my tooth had pierced it after he punched me in the face. I was almost unrecognizable, and she took care of me until I could care for myself.

****

Lisa had picked me up in the middle of the night, bloody and broken; Junior had passed out. She took me to her place, ran a hot bath and helped me wash the sticky blood out of my matted hair. We cried together without speaking, and I knew I would be safe while I was with her.

The next day she took me to the doctor after I lost the battle about not going, and she stayed with me while my arm was splinted, and I got stitches above my eye and near my left ear. She answered questions for me and got snippy with the doctor when he implied that I was not being truthful about what happened, even though he was right.

On the way back to her place, she stopped at the liquor store, picked up some wine and we drank all afternoon. We sat on her bedroom floor and finished two bottles while she did her best to cheer me up, solve my problems and distract me.

"That is a nasty habit," I said, as I watched her open the window and light a cigarette. Her apartment was on the seventh floor of a twelve-story building, and she often sat in the open window and smoked.

"I like it," she said. That was what she always said.

As I watched her light the cigarette and take her perch on the sill, I admired how sexy she looked, even smoking. She had a sensual aura as part of her personality anyway, but I think all the wine intensified my feelings for her.

"What?" she asked as she flicked her butt onto the unsuspecting people below.

"Nothing," I said, suddenly embarrassed that she caught me staring at her.

She poured us another glass and sat on the floor next to me. We leaned against the end of her bed and sat quietly for a little while. Then without warning she turned and kissed me. I am sure the alcohol had something to do with the flood of warmth I felt throughout my body, but I had never been kissed the way she kissed me. It was tender and slow, unrushed. Her lips were meaty and firm and the intentional way her hands were moving across my body created an overwhelming desire in me.

She helped me up and onto her bed where she gently laid me backwards onto her pillows. I felt calm and relaxed. It was probably the combination of pain meds and alcohol. The anticipation of what was coming made my body hot all over. Lisa slid partially on top of me, careful not to touch my splint. She reached across my back and carefully pulled me tightly against her so that we were both on our sides. She felt so good up against me and kissed my stitches and my bruises so tenderly that I was overwhelmed with love for her. She kissed my neck and slowly kissed her way up to my lips, sucking my skin gently at first and then more firmly. My body shuddered as I rolled onto my back and pulled her on top of me. When her tongue grazed across mine I reflexively arched into her and pulled her hard into me. She let out a deep moan, almost a growl, and we kissed deeply while she melted into me. We woke the next morning in the same position.

"Hey, sleepyhead," she said softly, rolling off me.

"Well. That was new." I yawned. I stretched my arms, curled up under the covers, and basked in complete contentment.

She laughed and left me alone while she ambled into the kitchen to make our coffee.

Oddly I would think to most people, nothing about our relationship changed. She was the emotional crutch I needed then, and her loyalty and kindness I could never completely understand. She made me feel that no matter what, she would always be there for me and we continued on, never feeling the need to talk about it.

****

"Well, well, ladies, this is quite the spectacle."

It was Mase, pouring himself and all of us a cup of coffee. I hadn't even noticed him.

"They are a sorry sight," offered Ad.

He placed the cups in front of both of us and we blindly grabbed until we grasped the handle and each took a gulp.

"This is almost exactly the same sight. . ." Ad Began.

"As the lawn fete incident." Mase finished.

Lawn fetes are big parties with games, rides and food and that also include a very large yard sale that are held as fundraisers on the grounds of churches in the Northeast. These parties also included alcohol tents.

"I'll never forget them in that three-legged race," Ad said.

"Drunk," Mase added.

"Buzzed," Lisa and I interjected together, not lifting our heads of the cool granite.

The guys hopped around the kitchen mocking how we supposedly looked and the fact that Lisa gets so competitive when I fell she wouldn't let me regain my balance and had to drag me across the finish line—and that we looked exactly like we did now, back then.

With their mocking over for the moment, the events of the night before slowly crept through my foggy brain until they were interrupted by a knock at the front door.

"Who would show up at this hour without calling?" Lisa whined, without moving or opening her eyes.

"It is eight o'clock," said Mase, extra loudly.

"It's Saturday," Ad said re-entering the kitchen after identifying the visitor. "It's Aideen."

"Oh God, I totally forgot she was coming today," Leese moaned, latching on to her cup.

Aideen was Greggins' mother, and even though she had stopped cleaning houses for a living many years ago when she got a good job working at the chicken plant, she kept a few regulars to make extra money. Saturdays at 8:00 was her regular time but in our stupor we had completely forgotten.

"I'm going home to take a nap," I pronounced, rising from the table and meandering toward the bedroom to gather my things.

"Good idea," Mase added, I'm sure Zoey will be up in a couple hours, and we haven't forgotten what day this is, have we?"

"Damn," Lisa and I said together. There would be no rest today.

Chapter 5

"Happy day you became a mom!"

Zoey burst through my bedroom door and jumped between Mase and me like she had done on every birthday since she was a little girl. We were prepared and clothed. A lesson learned early on. It was 11:30 and our nap was officially over.

"Happy day you were born, Zo." I turned over to kiss her cheek, morning breath and all.

"Happy birthday, Zenith," Mase added, kissing her other cheek.

"Enough with the formality," she said. "Where are my presents?"

"You know the deal," Mase said. "Presents tonight after the shoot."

She did know the deal. Her October birthday always fell around the time of opening day of dove season, and it had become traditional to celebrate it on that Saturday. Can't blame a girl for trying, though. I had recovered, barely, from my overindulgence at Lisa's, and grabbed any energy drink I left on the side table for this specific time.

Mase got dressed and hurried out to meet Ad and AJ to make final preparations for the big event. RJ picked up Z for some birthday shopping in the city, and Lisa, along with Mary Sue and some of the other gals, were coming over to help me with my own details.

****

The dove shoot began like it always did, on my man's family farm—a place that Senator Downes could use as a tax write-off, because in real life nothing about him screamed "I'm a farmer." The shoot had become a tradition over the years and was more of an excuse for fellowship and drinking than an actual event that would provide food for even one person—and the senator was never present. I think he thought allowing the collective to use his place gained goodwill, and in reality, it did.

This year there was more pressure to make it a successful hunt because some of Ad's current and potential political donors were attending, as well as some colleagues from the Senate flying in from Washington, DC, and this was his opportunity to sell himself to his peers and his constituents. He needed more money than ever for this upcoming campaign because he was running against a well-known and established political family. Senator Downes had offered this venue specifically to Ad for this event; we weren't sure why, could be for appearances sake, or he could have a plan of some sort— I mean it was annual event we were going to have anyway, but allowing Ad to use it as a fundraiser was certainly calculated for the senator's gain at some point. Now that he was out of prison, it seemed like he was everywhere. I was surprised that Ad accepted his offer, for a few reasons, but the obvious was that people in Banjoland are somewhat unpredictable, and there was really no way to control how they would behave. Ad would be taking a risk exposing the more sophisticated political crowd to the home group that lacked much worldly experience. Not to allege that the locals were politically naïve; to the contrary, they were very aware of who voted for and against legislation that affected their livelihood. They simply lacked cultural sophistication, or as Mase would say, they could smell the bullshit and were vocal when they did. In any case, Ad said that his colleagues had been curious about his life in the South and at the same time, he said, he wanted to position himself as a man who could appeal to all voting blocks for possible future use, including the Southern outdoorsman.

Mase and Ad had been preparing for this event for several weeks, planting and grooming fields, careful to follow all the laws and rules that covered dove hunting and reminding the regular guys that there would be no hunting over a baited field.

"Damn," Billy Joe piped up, as he stood beside the burn barrel still in his grease-covered jeans and shirt and slurping his seventh Busch Light. "How are we supposed to get anything that way?"

"At least this time you'll have an excuse when you come back empty-handed," Mase offered, gulping down a foreign import.

****

It was late in the afternoon, on schedule, when the caravan of black Cadillacs mixed with pristine late model trucks, also black, proceeded slowly up the long, tree-covered dirt drive. I almost laughed out loud at the absurdity of this sight. It looked more like a funeral procession than a dove shoot. Greggins McGreggor was standing at the top of the driveway, his shoulder length orange ringlets an obvious contrast to his camo overalls, directing each vehicle into a row so they would be able to exit quickly and easily.

Mental Note: Greggins stature and his level of

*maturity made him fit right in with Z, RJ and the rest of
their friends, even though he was a few years younger.
RJ bonded with him, I think, over the fact that neither
had a father in their lives and I thought that was really
nice.*

The gals stayed back to entertain the wives. I would
have much preferred to be in the truck with Mase, but I
knew I was expected as a hostess of this event to make
sure everyone had a good time, so I didn't even question
my relegation to mingling.

As the afternoon progressed into early evening and
the wine was free flowing, I began to learn a lot about
the ladies in my charge. A few of them were with their
husbands solely for the purpose of deflating the egos of
their husbands' girlfriends. And while I'm not a naïve
person in any sense, the fact that they so openly
commiserated about this, in front of strangers, did
surprise me.

"It's because we're all women," Leese proffered.
"We all understand."

As dusk fell and the men began to return, beer
bottles and dove feathers bouncing in the backs of the
trucks, Greggins approached me to ask about the band.

"Ms. Lanie, the band is here. Do you want them to
set up?"

We didn't usually have a band at this event, but
Mase decided that we should splurge in consideration of
the importance of the occasion. Plus, it helped that it
could also be part of Zoey's birthday gift. After a brief
discussion, Greggins directed the musicians to their
assigned location under the remodeled pavilion. It
wasn't long before they were in full swing. and Zoey, RJ,
and their friends were line dancing like they were

auditioning for a reality show. They wore cowboy hats and boots—Standard Banjoland fare—Greggins had a piece of straw hanging out of his mouth circa *Hee Haw*, camo overalls and a straw hat to complete his ensemble.

Mental Note: Take video to show Z's children one day

Lisa, sitting on a nearby tailgate and peering through her binoculars at random people in the crowd around us, offered commentary and opinion, until she uttered "uo-oh" and handed me the field glasses.

It was unmistakable. The large white dooly (those oversized trucks with 6 wheels) with the fancy gold D outlined in black slowly made its way towards us from the bottom of the driveway until it stopped next to the bandstand and he emerged, wearing a black cowboy hat and boots. He was an imposing figure who chatted and shook hands on his way towards us. I couldn't think of a legitimate reason for him to show up at this event, other than to be seen, but that question was answered when he produced a small white envelope, an invitation, addressed to Mase and me for lunch the next day at the club.

"Odd," Mase said when I showed it to him later that evening, "a literal, personal invitation. This is new."

"Especially because your mother made a point of texting the other day inviting us and insisting we be there. Why the formality?"

"I guess we will see tomorrow."

Chapter 6

We stood formally next to the table waiting for Olivia to acknowledge us before we took our seats, and I couldn't help but wonder why we were summoned for this special meeting. Maybe we could wipe the slate clean and start fresh.

Olivia glanced up from her conversation and without any hesitation offered her hand to Mase. She nodded and held her hand towards the open chairs encouraging us to sit.

"Mother, you look wonderful," Mase offered, as he pulled out my chair.

"Yes, Olivia," I added, "you look terrific, almost glowing." I was proud of my effort.

She smiled but did not speak. She glanced across the room as if she were waiting for someone, but the senator had texted his regrets due to an "unforeseen business matter."

Suddenly there was a collective gasp and the ancillary noise faded immediately into the background as an alluring, olive skinned beauty scanned the crowd until her eyes fixated on Mase. The timbre of the moment immediately changed.

The fashionable red dress she was wearing accentuated her curves and displayed her cleavage in a visible, but tasteful way. She had glossed and styled shoulder length dark brown hair and long bangs that glided across her forehead against eyes that were very light blue. The way the old-fashioned lighting illuminated her olive complexion and facial features made her seem ethereal. She was stunning.

"Bella!" said Mase as soon as their eyes connected. He dropped my hand and ran to her like she was a longsuffering love and he was returning from war. He hugged her with abandon, and she returned it flirtatiously, leaning into him and bending her leg upwardly, seductively, like a 1950s pinup girl. Olivia observed this smugly, not remotely hiding her pleasure at this scene.

I had no idea who she was, but obviously there had been something between this woman and my husband. His uninhibited response to her caught me off guard.

After the world's longest hug, he stood up straight, took a step back, and apparently recalled the fact that he was married, swung around to see my confused look, hands awkwardly in my lap.

"Lanie, sweetie, come here, I want you to meet someone," he said, unable to control his excitement.

"Sure." I took his offered hand tightly, suddenly more self-conscious than I had ever been with him.

"Sweetie, I'd like you to meet Annabella. Well, I call her Bella." He smiled at her.

He calls her Bella.

I felt an unexpected pang in my heart. Who was this exotic, sexy woman and why did she have this effect on my husband?

"Bella, this is my lovely wife, Lanie."

"Hey," I said as I mustered my most pleasant smile and reached my hand out toward her, hoping the sweat had completely dried. "It's nice to meet you."

She stepped toward me and before I could prepare myself, she hugged me. Not the side hug used for the opposite sex or for those with whom we aren't familiar, but a full frontal.

I was rattled but did my best to hide my discomfort.

"It's so very nice to meet you," she said, sounding sincere and with an accent that I placed somewhere in the Mediterranean. We smiled at each other briefly while Mase stood over us like he was creating a reunion of old friends.

The look on his face when his eyes met hers was a look that I had only seen him show for me. Welcoming, loving, adoring...I felt like I had been punched. Like in middle school when you liked a boy, really liked him, and then found out he was secretly mocking you to his friends. Or then in high school, when by some remote chance the popular guy pretended to like you, and for a moment you convinced yourself that you really were pretty and that of course he liked you, but then you found out he was just pretending to win a bet with his buddies about whether he could get you into bed and take your ultimate prize. And then with Junior...the supposed "one." The one who betrayed me in inventive and creative ways that no matter how hard I tried to understand always seemed to be my fault. In his one look, all the insecurities I thought I had banished from my being reappeared.

This was why Olivia wanted to meet us here. She had arranged this encounter.

"Bella, why don't you join us?" Olivia crowed.

"Yes! You must join us," Mase added, giddy with emotion.

"Well, I don't want to interrupt," Bella said in her

sultry from somewhere other than here accent.

"Nonsense," said Mase, "you must join us."

And so she did.

She was friendly and sophisticated, but who was she to him? Was anyone going to explain?

"So tell me, Lanie," she said, oozing interest and hospitality, "what brings a girl from New York City down South to Clarkesville, of all places?"

She seemed sincere and it aggravated me. Despite an unfeigned effort, I couldn't find anything wrong with what she said or how she behaved. She seemed to be a genuinely nice person.

"It's not a very interesting story," I recounted, "job. . . best friend. . . needed a change."

"You must miss it," she interrupted. "Life here is so boring and slow..." and then noticing the pained look on Mase's face, she abruptly stopped speaking. After a moment, she rephrased, "What I mean is that living here isn't for everyone."

Mental Note: What the hell is going on?

Since no one seemed eager to fill in the blanks for me, I took it upon myself to do it.

"So spill," I said, to no one in particular. "What's the story between you two?" I asked as a polite inquiry but needing an answer.

Olivia held up her hand and immediately her glass was re-filled, and her cigarette lit by a gloved hand from the shadows. She had a prime seat for this unscripted drama, and she digested every word that was said back and forth in silence, like it was a volley at Wimbledon.

Bella looked confused.

"You didn't tell her about us?" she asked. She looked hurt.

39

Mase spoke quickly. "We dated in college, you know. Then we graduated and went our separate ways."

Bella looked down and took a sip of her Chardonnay.

This was Olivia's chance. Carpe diem!

She swirled her wine deliberately, took a drink and broke the silence.

"You haven't shared with Melanie that you and lovely Bella were engaged, dear?" She drew a long drag from her cigarette while this nugget of information hung in the air. Point Olivia.

"No need, Mother," he said with certainty. "The relationship I had with Bella is in the past and I am fortunate to have found the woman for me."

Point Mase.

Then it struck me. Olivia's revenge had begun. Instinctively I knew there were troubled waters ahead.

Chapter 7

"Wow," he said, still breathing heavily. "That was great!"

It *was* great. Sex with him was always good and sometimes great, but the passion in his touch and kiss this morning was different. It was more aggressive, more desperate...more passionate.

I smiled and ran my fingers leisurely over his toned abs, following the muscular curve inward and down between his legs. He responded immediately. I was surprised that he was ready again so quickly. He flipped me over and mounted me in one motion, ejaculating after four strokes.

"Sorry," he said sheepishly.

"No worries," I replied, quickly scrounging for my t-shirt and panties. I suddenly felt the need to get away from him. That was the strangest love making session we'd ever had.

I let the steamy shower water cascade over my body while I shaved my legs and wondered about Annabella and what my man thought about her return. I wasn't naïve enough to think our sexual interlude didn't have anything to do with her, but I also wondered why she was back, and more importantly, for how long. The fact that I even had these questions irritated me. I didn't want to have questions about anything significant. I didn't want to hear justifications, explanations, and I did not want to

41

worry. I was finally at a point in my life where things were good. No, not good. They were great. Mase and I were an excellent match, physically and emotionally. We laughed at people who took life too seriously, and we enjoyed every day. We were still trying to get pregnant and granted, we were both frustrated that it hadn't happened yet, but there were options if we needed to move in that direction. Zoey was an outgoing, fun teen whose spunkiness added to the texture of our lives. She was the only tangible souvenir from my relationship with Junior; otherwise that life would have belonged to someone else. Given that we had survived Junior's return, the accident, the trial and a host of lesser events, we should be able to handle the return of my husband's ex–girlfriend. . .fiancée. . . ex-fiancée.

I toweled off and caught a glimpse of hair and flesh in the mirror. I stopped, dropped the towel to the floor and took a minute to look at myself. I slowly examined my naked reflection, starting with my curly wet hair (always curly when wet) and freshly scrubbed face. I was in my early thirties, but my face had no visible wrinkles or crow's feet, thanks to a good skin care regimen imported from NYC. My copper-colored eyes were framed by dark brown, long eyelashes and manicured brows. I had a proportioned, athletic build and curves where they should be with defined arms and shoulders. My skin was tan, left over from summer, with freckles, but not too many. I decided I looked good for me and avoided direct comparisons to Bella. I found myself paying extra attention to my makeup as I blended the matte powder across my cheekbones, careful to avoid streaks. I wondered if she was paying extra attention to her makeup this morning. Whatever her intent, there was no way I was going to let her disrupt the happiness I worked so hard to create for my family, and I knew instinctively that something was going on and it would eventually be revealed. But for the moment, I would remain rational and secure, at least outwardly, and I would not overreact. I would definitely not overreact.

I wandered, displaying my best after shower look, and found Mase in the kitchen scrambling eggs and whistling some tune I vaguely recognized, emphasizing the chorus by slapping to the beat on the empty egg carton.

"Breakfast, my lady." He plopped the plate down theatrically with an exaggerated bow.

"So, Mase," I began. I couldn't help it. I needed details.

"She left me," he interjected, clearly anticipating this conversation.

"She left you?"

"Yes. We were engaged and supposed to be married after we graduated from college. I know I probably should have mentioned her, but I saw no point. That was a long time ago and I have moved on. Obviously."

Obviously.

"So, she just left?"

"Yes," he said, plainly trying to keep any emotional attachment to what he was saying under control and remain upbeat. "We were planning the wedding and she left a note saying she couldn't live here anymore, that she felt smothered and that she needed to find herself. I probably should have seen it coming, but I thought having a husband and family would fulfill her. I was wrong."

I let those words settle for a minute before I

responded. "I'm so sorry, Mase. That must have been terribly painful for you."

I held his hand to my cheek and kissed his fingers tenderly. That woman hurt him deeply, despite his manly attempt to minimize his feelings. But it was also apparent he was extremely glad to see her. More than glad, overjoyed would be my description.

"Not a big deal," he said. "I'm over it. Eat your eggs before they get cold."

****

"Should I be worried, Leese?"

I was not going to overreact in front of Mase under any circumstances and if anyone would tell me the truth, Lisa would.

"Yes," she said without hesitation. "I mean, I don't want to stress you out, but I have been giving it a lot of thought." She continued, "Why is she here? How long is she staying? Why did she show up last night? Is Olivia paying her?"

I thought about the small envelope I saw Olivia giving who I was now sure was Bella in the parking lot that night at the football game. I swirled the orange juice and champagne in my glass. These were exactly the questions I had been asking myself.

"Something doesn't feel right," she added. "I don't trust her, and I don't think you should either." She took a drink from her chilled flute.

"Olivia obviously has her back here for some reason, and I think it's to cause disruption in your relationship and pay you back for everything. I mean why else would she come back?"

This was an angle I never expected. I didn't know Mase had a serious love relationship before me and I

44

guess I never thought seriously about Olivia's revenge. I mean, revenge is such an antiquated principle.

Lisa and I continued to drink and chat about our relationships back in the day, first about her and Ad, and how they met in a co-ed volleyball league and short little Lisa spiked the ball right into Ad and broke his nose, then about me and Mase, and how odd it was for me to meet someone I loved in Banjoland, and how you just never knew how these things would happen. Lisa turned on the radio and a vaguely familiar voice was singing some depressing refrain in a baritone country twang.

"Remember?" Leese snorted, her eyes glistening like they did when she drank just enough. "Remember?" she almost shouted. She slapped AJ's worn cowboy hat onto her chestnut hair and belted out random words into the empty champagne flute she was using as a microphone, badly, along with the radio. "Who am I?" she asked.

I had no idea whom she was imitating, but she looked hilarious swaying back and forth, singing into her glass along with the melody.

"Maybe this will help." She laughed as she turned down the radio and cleared her throat.

She "sang" out in her best soprano attempt, replete with Southern accent, "*Islands in the stream, that is what we are, no one in between...",* the Dolly Parton and Kenny Rogers hit.

"I did not look like that, and I sounded a hell of a lot better."

We laughed and reminisced about the time I sang this song and did karaoke with Blake Shelton at my bachelorette party. He was touring country bars to get footage for a country music video, and I had no idea who he was until my friends educated me. He couldn't believe I had never heard of him and dragged me to the floor to sing a duet. I proceeded to tell him I was surprised he made a living singing and he laughed and said, "only in America."

Lisa and I continued to drink and talk and share the ease of each other's presence until late in the afternoon.

****

"I'm sorry," he said. "I really am."

Images of Bella laughing joyfully flashed around his head like fireworks exploding. I screamed questions at him. "What about our marriage?" "What about Z?" "I thought you loved me!"

I panicked at the thought of losing him and our family.

"Lanie, honey, wake up." Mase shook me gently.

I recoiled at his touch while my eyes focused. I was filled with panic, and my heart was pounding inside my chest.

"It's okay," he said. "You were having a bad dream."

I met his eyes and saw the tenderness and compassion that helped me fall in love with him. This kind, loving man was mine. I reached for his hand and put it on my chest over my heart so he could feel it racing from this awful dream. I kissed him tenderly and my love began to expand. I was desperate to show him how I felt—that I was thankful for him and our life. He slid my hand over the swelling in his pants and I unzipped him, freeing his passion to share with me.

We made love in a fierce and intentional way, grasping each other like it was the last time we would ever be romantically together. We orgasmed simultaneously as I held his bicep tightly with both of my hands and rested my head on his shoulder as he drifted off and began to lightly snore. I sniffed in his scent and prayed I could return to a dreamless, peaceful sleep.

When I woke in the morning he was gone—which wasn't unusual, though today it made me feel a little uneasy.

I chastised myself for what I hoped was unnecessary worry, even though I was smart enough to know that Bella was back with a purposeful intent and it wasn't to insure my happiness. Mase had given me no reason to doubt him or us . . . it was the look on Olivia's face that haunted me.

Chapter 8

I waited, anxiously, because I knew this time was different. . . I just had a feeling. I occupied myself for the required two minutes by checking my twitter feed and scanning Instagram. What if this time was different? Would it be? One more time I imagined what our family would be like if Mase and I had a physical expression of our love.

I very slowly let myself look. I had done this so often it was almost routine. It was like "Let's Make a Deal" and I was slowly pulling back the curtain, hoping for the grand prize, but instead received the consolation—the Walmart gift card. I had been numbed and conditioned to expect the same sterile, unfeeling "thanks for playing" response every time. And now it felt like for the umpteenth time I was going through the motions just so I could report that I did, in fact "take the test." We had been trying earnestly for so long now that when we spoke about it we were overtly supportive and encouraging with each other and at the same time I could feel simmering and muted frustration that it hadn't already happened for us. But now, could it really be happening? I stared at the blue plus sign in disbelief, imagining how our lives were going to change and how this was going to secure our happiness. I could barely contain myself as I called Leese with the news.

"Shut up! Really?" said Leese.

"Yep! I am. I really am. I'm pregnant."

It felt weird hearing myself say the words out loud.

She knew we had been trying, but she always let me bring up the subject first, and she never pried. She didn't have to; I shared everything with her.

"Did you tell Mase?" she asked.

"No, you first," I said. "I'm planning on telling him tonight after I pick up his favorites from the Piggly Wiggly Deli (as close as I come to cooking). Then we'll tell Z together. She will flip."

"I know. She's been on a baby rant since you got married," Lisa recounted. "I am happy for you, my friend, we will celebrate soon. Call me after you tell Mase. I want all the deets."

Naturally I would. I was beside myself with happiness and expectation.

****

I spent the afternoon cleaning up, rearranging things, and ruminating about the exact way I should tell him our family was expanding. Should I hint and give clues and let him guess? Should I just blurt it out? I decided to play it by ear and lit the candles just as he pulled into the driveway.

"Hey, babe," I said flirtatiously, "how was your day?"

"Good." He pecked me on the cheek.

Oddly, he didn't mention the candles or the tablecloth—things that were obviously out of the ordinary.

"Nice spread," he offered as he took his place at the table.

I was barely able to contain myself and was about to blurt out my news when he pushed himself back a little and slid his chair around the table until he was right next to me. He took my hands in his.

"I have news," he said.

"Me, too!" I exclaimed. I couldn't wait to tell him he was going to be a father.

"I don't know how to say this, so I'm just going to say it," he said softly. "I am a father. I have a son."

How could he know? I hadn't told him anything yet. "What?"

He squeezed my hands tightly, almost as if he were holding me in place.

"I am a father," he repeated. "Bella has a son and I am his father. He is twelve years old."

He talked like he was reading me an article from his phone, like he was reporting random information that had no effect on us personally. He added before I asked, "I did not know."

I freaked on the inside.

I didn't speak as I tried to make sense of his words. I could feel the panic swelling inside me. I could feel my heart racing as all kinds of thoughts popped into my mind like uninvited party guests. This was going to change everything.

I pulled my hands from his quickly, like I had been shocked by an electric current.

I was enraged and felt betrayed, even though in my mind, I knew this happened before I had ever met Mase. That didn't really matter. The anger I felt was so overwhelming I almost couldn't control it. How dare she pop into our lives, especially now that we were finally going to have a baby—our baby. Now it was too late. He already had one. With someone else.

I did what I always do when I am hurt or angry, or

betrayed. I shut down completely. I was raging and furious and hurt. I had so many feelings and thoughts competing for my attention, it was inner chaos. The only clue about how I was feeling to those on the outside was the coldness I knew that radiated from my eyes, like a laser.

"Lanie, honey, talk to me." He tried to wrap me in his arms and hold me, but I would not let him. All I could think about was him and Bella and their son. I did not want him to touch me.

****

"You didn't tell him?" Lisa asked.

"I couldn't," I said, glad I had retreated to her house with Z in tow so she could take AJ for his bi-weekly haircut.

Zoey loved spending time with Lisa, but even more so now that AJ was a young boy and not a toddler. It was funny how maternal she was with him, and whenever she was around, he was her shadow.

"You're going to need to talk to him, to figure out what y'all are going to do," said Leese.

"I know."

I didn't have to talk to him to know that he was going to take an active part in his son's life. That's the kind of guy he is, and I wouldn't respect him otherwise.

"You know this is Olivia's doing, right?" Lisa offered.

"I hardly think Olivia slept with Bella," I responded sarcastically.

"Duh. Why did Bella decide after twelve years to announce she's a baby mama?" Lisa asked while she poured some champagne for us. Then, remembering, she poured my glass into hers until it overflowed a little.

Lisa knew I despised the words baby mama and baby daddy, no matter how apropos. She was right, though. Why would Bella show up now? Olivia had struck hard and unexpectedly. This was it, her perfect revenge.

Chapter 9

He couldn't have been more considerate of my feelings, and I did everything I could to be supportive and encouraging; any venting I did was to Lisa.

"Do you think I should tell him about *our* baby?" I asked.

"Definitely. He loves you and it's not like he isn't going to find out eventually anyway, so choose your timing."

I knew she was right. Deep inside I knew Mase loved me, but I also knew how much he wanted a child and obviously whatever feelings he had for Bella were not completely dead.

"I'm scared, Leese. I don't want to share him or our family with her. I want to take the high road, but I don't think I can."

She took my hand gently in hers and looked directly into my eyes. "It's going to be okay," she said, "eventually."

I almost believed her.

****

It did not take very long for the changes to happen. Longer and more frequent visits to get to know his son. West. That is his name. I was surprised by this. Officially named Mason Westhoven Downes V but called West. Every time I thought about this boy having my husband's name I felt like I was kicked in the gut. But I was determined to adjust to this situation and be as supportive as possible, so that Mase could develop a positive relationship with his boy.

Over time their visits grew into baseball games and ice cream outings, and they all included Bella (and sometimes me, although I tried to respect their need for one-on-one time), who was tagging along, "just in case West gets a little uncomfortable," she said. Mase included me, and West seemed like a nice kid, but it was obvious, at least to me, that Bella's intentions included more than a father and son reunion.

I was just beginning my second trimester and decided, now that I knew my pregnancy would likely go full term, that I would tell Mase the news by making him the one thing I could cook: breakfast for supper. His favorite was a meat filled omelet, sausage and hash browns with peppers and onions.

"Hey, Melanie," Bella said, when I unexpectedly ran into her while shopping for my supper ingredients at the Piggly Wiggly. She didn't look like someone who did her own grocery shopping, evidenced by her asking me where to find Almond Milk—the milk that Mase drinks. She was a fool if she thought I was going to disappear out of his life, and though I didn't know if she had made overt gestures toward Mase or not, if she hadn't, I knew it wouldn't be long until she did.

"Hey, Bella," I said, glad I made the decision for full makeup on this trip. "It's over along the far wall with the dairy products." I pointed as I continued down the aisle, acting completely undisturbed by this encounter.

****

I was surprisingly calm and relaxed as we chatted over breakfast/supper. Mase scarfed down his food like it was his last meal.

"That was fantastic," he said, wiping his face and picking up our plates to take to the sink. "What's this?" He picked up the folded ultrasound I had hidden beneath his plate.

"Is this—"

"Yes!" I interrupted before he could finish his sentence. "Yes! We're having a baby!"

An enormous grin crept across his face until his silly, toothy smile beamed his approval. He practically dropped our plates back onto the table and pulled me out of my chair and into his arms.

"We're having a baby!" He hugged me tightly, and then abruptly stopped. "Oh, I'm sorry, honey, I don't want to squeeze too hard."

I laughed, relieved and happy, and we kissed tenderly and deeply. For the first time since Bella's appearance, I felt like things were going to be okay.

****

News of our joy spread quickly, as all information in Banjoland does, and it wasn't long before the calls and texts began.

Zoey was thrilled and because she was my child, never really attempted to filter what she thought.

"Mom," she said once we squealed together and she expressed that it was about time because she wasn't getting any younger, "how do you think *she* is going to handle the news?"

Z always referred to Bella as "she" when she spoke to me about her because she thought Bella was an interloper and didn't trust her intentions. Zoey was polite and appropriate in public, because she was a Southern girl by geography and training, and this was how one was to behave in public despite how one truly feels.

"I don't know, Z, Mase is officially telling her tonight when he picks up West, though I'm sure she's already heard."

"I don't trust her, Mom."

"I know, babe. Neither do I and neither does Leese."

Mase reported that Bella took the news in stride, offering congratulations and support, which is more than we received from his mother.

"You already have a son. Why on earth would you possibly want another child?" she'd asked when he broke the news. He didn't tell me this at first, but I pressed him for details because my intuition told me she and Bella were in collusion. Not to mention that he adopted Zoey when she was a little girl, so technically he had two children with one on the way.

"Don't worry about what Mother thinks," he'd said. "Her opinion doesn't matter, and I am thrilled."

And he was thrilled. It was obvious in everything he did. We painted the nursery together; he researched formula and baby food and toys and schools—even colleges. He treated me like a queen, and it made me love him more. Oddly, his father hadn't said anything to either of us about it and we had seen him a few times at the Club since it became common knowledge we were expecting. I really didn't care though. Mase was doing a terrific job of balancing our life with incorporating West, and my only concern was that Bella was always around. Even if we took West to dinner as a family, she would appear at the same place, allegedly coincidentally.

****

We pulled into the crowded parking lot of the only OB/GYN practice in town—Mase assured me they were competent—and piled out of the truck like it was a Saturday morning outing at the flea market—a joke we had about Banjoland's premier trading center. Every Saturday morning multitudes of people from the Tri-County area would descend on the flea market to find the deals, and when Mase and Leese were trying to explain the draw it had on people, they likened it to an *outside* Walmart and then I understood, kind of.

After several minutes in the waiting room and a few minutes to change into the gown and get into the familiar position. Dr. Fisher and his cute twentyish ultrasound tech, fresh out of ultrasound school, entered the room laughing and greeted me with a hearty, "Good to see. . .all of you?"

We decided to make the revelation of the sex of our child a family affair, so Leese and Z were with us. We offered to bring West as well, but Bella said he had other plans.

Lisa sat in the corner on one of those rolling stools looking at a *Today's Woman* magazine and Zoey was texting someone on her phone. Mase stood beside me holding my hand and staring at the monitor until the doctor finished taking my vital signs and then nodded for Z to join us for the reveal. "Ready?" he asked.

We nodded in sync as Dr. Fisher stood next to Julie the tech and she put the lubricant across my belly. It was cold and it briefly brought back a memory of when I was pregnant with Z and how disappointed Junior was to find out he was having a girl.

"Okay, here we go." Julie slipped the wand across the little bulge in my stomach. "Let's see what we have."

Immediately we heard its racing heartbeat that verified she or he was alive, and I surprised myself as I began to cry. Dr. Fisher gave Julie some instruction regarding where to move the wand and then he suddenly pushed down on my side and nodded at the screen. We could see the outline of a tiny baby, fully formed.

"Can you tell what it is?" I asked. This was the entire purpose of our visit.

"Yes," Mase practically yelled. "Look right there." He pointed to a specific oblong, shaded area on the monitor. "See," he said, "that's a penis. It's a boy."

Dr. Fisher and the tech chuckled.

"I hate to disappoint you," she said, "but that's the baby's arm."

Leese chimed in, "High expectations, there, don't ya think?"

The tech continued to roll the wand around a little, occasionally stopping to push a little.

"Here we go," she said.

We looked closely but it was hard to see anything definitive.

"What is it?" I asked, squinting.

"Right here." She pointed with her finger to show us the tiniest extremity.

"That's his penis. It *is* a boy."

Dr. Fisher smiled and nodded to confirm.

"It *is* a boy!" Mase exclaimed and squeezed my hand tightly. He kissed me, like this was my accomplishment, and then immediately turned to Z and said, "Naturally I want a boy. I already have a girl who broke the mold."

She smiled at him in return and she and Leese gathered around Mase to see the penis.

Lisa chuckled and added, "Well, by the size of things, it looks like your son certainly takes after you."

Chapter 10

"What are the rules?" Leese asked during our weekly walk on the nature trail. It used to be our every other day run but running had become uncomfortable for me as my pregnancy progressed. I like being on the trail because it was shaded by large oak trees and there was a small creek that ran along it with large rocks where we could sit and chat if we felt like it. It was a very peaceful place where animals and people freely mingled.

"I really don't know," I replied, stepping over a root in the path. "Doesn't the child have to be born in the context of marriage to legitimately carry on a family name?

It didn't matter, Bella had already named West after Mase and it wouldn't do any good to waste time simmering over something we couldn't change. It was actually Mase who mentioned the name situation later on in that week.

"I've been giving some thought to our son's name," he offered during our evening "catch up" time on the porch.

"Me too." I nodded.

"Let me say that I love West, but I always thought our child would carry on my name. Since that can't happen, and I *am* sorry about that, I have another idea."

I listened as he continued.

"I always thought I would want to keep the legacy

of my name going by passing it on from me to my son to his son. But after I really thought about it, my father kind of ruined what I thought our name stood for. And what I mean by that is I am just not as invested in that idea as I once was. So this is what I suggest: I think we should combine both our names and start a new legacy for our children."

I thought about that for a minute and then I knew what he meant. It was commonplace in Southern families to combine the mother's maiden name with the father's surname to create a blending of the families. In our case that would mean our son's name would be Clark Downes.

"I love it," I said, "but I have one suggestion."

He nodded for me to continue.

"I'd like to name him Mason Clark Downes, and we can call him Clark."

And it was settled. Our son had a name.

Chapter 11

I was simply trying to help. Mase was in the shower when his phone rang, so I thought I would answer, as we both do for each other, and tell whoever was calling he'd get back to them as soon as he could.

I didn't recognize the name on the caller ID; it simply read "I.M." and I didn't give it much thought. I answered but no one responded, and I assumed the call was dropped. That was until I heard the sound his phone makes when he receives a text message. It was from I.M.

"You tell her, or I will."

My heart shrank. And I did what any woman would do and scrolled back through his texts.

It couldn't have been worse. It didn't take long for me to figure out that I.M. was Bella and to remember her name is Isabella Manzanarres.

It was obvious they had slept together from her text: "last night was just like old times and you're as good as always" with three heart emojis following it. He did not respond to it. From the date of the text, it was two weeks ago. When we were naming our son. Between the thoughts of divorcing him and the anger at his betrayal, I completely lost my mind.

He was singing some old rock classic steaming up the bathroom with the heat from the shower, which normally I found cute. I flung open the shower curtain and threw the phone so hard at him it broke into pieces and fell with the water toward the drain.

I screamed at him. "How could you do this?"

He looked shocked and a little scared.

"Get out!" I screamed at him. I was hysterical.

He stumbled out of the shower and grabbed my arm. "Honey, what is it?"

"Really? Did you think I wouldn't find out?"

I was raging and I wouldn't let him near me.

"Lanie, wait, just let me explain," he begged while he was trying to keep a towel around his naked body. He reached for me again, but I shrugged him off.

"I said get out!" I growled at him.

"I am so sorry," he said, "please let me explain."

"Oh, okay," I said sarcastically. "Explain why you took off your clothes until you were naked and had sex with someone else. Go ahead."

"It was one time, and it was a huge mistake and I never wanted you to know because it didn't mean anything," he rambled.

They had a few drinks after West went to bed and one thing led to another. I stopped listening after that.

I felt numb.

"Lanie, I am so sorry, honey. Please, please, say something."

The tears were a nice touch. He looked sincerely sorry—almost distraught. I'm not even sure why he so readily admitted it—I thought part of cheating including automatic denials until the perp was faced with evidence. Unless he thought she would really tell me.

"Get your shit and get out." That was all I could say. I felt anxious and scared. Like life as I knew it was over.

No one expected me to end it with him except Leese, because she was the only one in my life who truly knew how I would react to such disloyalty and betrayal. Zoey pleaded with me to give him another chance, but I couldn't. I was so hurt and so angry that he let this happen that I wouldn't even consider it. And to make it even worse, I was pregnant for God's sake. Pregnant and crushed.

"Aren't you even gonna fight for your marriage, Mom?" Zoey asked.

"Why? Why would I want to be married to someone who cheats on me?"

"Well, you're just giving him to her, then." She huffed off to her room.

I knew this. But I also knew myself, and I wasn't sure if I would ever get over this betrayal enough to let it go and never bring it up again, and I knew that would be the only way we would ever be able to go forward.

Chapter 12

Lisa met me around 8:00 on the following Saturday morning, with a roll of duct tape and a few boxes she had salvaged from the Piggly Wiggly.

She hugged me tightly, for a long time. I needed to feel close to her, the one person I could trust before I took a breath and began the task at hand.

"Don't you think you might be acting too rashly?" she asked, as she followed me back to our bedroom where I had several boxes already packed.

"I can't look at him and this is all I know to do. Even if it's wrong, I have to do something."

She accepted that answer but added, "Olivia wins if you do it this way."

"Where do you want to start packing?" I asked, ignoring her perfectly legitimate comment.

It didn't take as long as you might think to pack up almost eight years of marriage. Except for the occasional meltdown over a picture, or a memento of some kind, we made fast progress. By noon we had all his things boxed and on the porch. I refused to talk to him and took the position that he was dead to me. It might seem extreme, but it was the only way I could cope.

****

RJ and Zoey returned from a trip to Tallahassee, where they bought some stuff for his dorm room so he would be ready when the time came for him to leave for

Florida State and, really, it was just an excuse for her to shop. I updated her on what my plan was before she left, but when she saw the boxes on the porch she started crying and begged me not to be in such a hurry.

"Can't you just wait a little while, Mom?" she pleaded. "I'm sure it won't take him long to figure out how to fix this."

My sweet, naïve child. It was no longer about whether he wanted me or not. I had removed myself from consideration. It was the only way I could function. Even Leese kept trying to discourage me from acting too quickly, but I knew that for me to survive I had to dismount the emotional roller coaster of trying to figure out why this happened and take control of my life. And that meant I had to cut off all feelings for Mase. Today was the beginning.

"I texted him," Leese said.

"And?" I said, and then immediately regretted acting interested.

"And he thinks you are acting impulsively. On the other hand, he understands." She was always a fan of his. "I told him what you said—that you would have all of his stuff hauled off to the Goodwill if he didn't get it today, and he said he would come by later this afternoon."

****

The sound of a door slamming woke me. I had fallen asleep not long after Lisa left, because I had barely been able to sleep a few hours at a time since his revelation. Getting his stuff out of my house was the final step before I could move on without him. This cut had been deeper than any other in my life and I needed to remove myself from the knife to stop the pain.

I glanced out the window and saw Mase's truck in the drive. I crept quietly to the front door and turned the lock. I slid the curtain open so there was a small slit that allowed me to see onto the porch without being seen myself.

He headed toward the door, but he must have thought better of it because he stopped, took a step backwards and sat on the bench. He reached for one of the boxes and slowly pulled back the tape. I recognized immediately the clunky frame he lifted out and held in his lap. It was a present to us for our first anniversary from Z. She had been so proud when she presented it to us that morning before she went to school. It was wrapped in toilet paper and inside a zip lock baggy that she had colored with markers, a chunky frame made from deer antlers sawed off at the tips. Mase was so touched that he immediately searched for a picture of all of us to put in it and displayed it prominently on the mantle, where it remained until this morning.

He held the frame against his chest for a couple of minutes while a few tears fell down his cheek and onto his hand. I let the curtain slowly close.

Chapter 13

The days turned into weeks and his calls and texts became fewer. I was emotional from the pregnancy and I was emotional from Mase's betrayal and I was emotional because Zoey was emotional about RJ's emotions about leaving for college later in the year. I avoided Mase and distracted myself with work, writing and planning for my son.

****

I was surprised it hadn't happened already. It wasn't like Banjoland was overly large and now that it was fall, it was basketball season (for the kids that didn't play football) and I was attending AJ's games. All the basketball teams used the same courts on the same days, so it wasn't surprising that Bella would be there with West. He was only a few years older than AJ, and if he played basketball like I heard he golfed, he would be the kid everyone talked about.

I wasn't sure, but I kind of expected I would see her since Leese told me she saw West practicing sometimes when she brought AJ to the courts. It made sense, because all the boys in Banjoland played sports during the week and hunted on the weekend, their age notwithstanding.

I rubbed my blush in upward strokes, sure to blend it smoothly with my foundation. I took extra care to apply my mascara so there would be no clumping, and I spent twenty-five minutes choosing my outfit in anticipation of our chance meeting. I was barely showing at 6 months, and I felt like I looked pretty good considering. Our encounter was just as awkward as anyone might think.

Lisa and I arrived first, according to plan, because I wanted to be seated in the bleachers surrounded by people we knew. I'm not sure why that was important to me save for the security of friends, I guess. It had been many years since Bella and Mase were engaged, but people in town still recognized and welcomed her.

We had been seated for about fifteen minutes, and I was surprisingly relaxed. They, the happy family, as I sarcastically referred to them when I was talking to Leese, came strolling up and West ran over to see his friends behind the bench on the opposite side of the gym. He really was a handsome boy, and I could see why Mase was proud of him. He was polite and seemed sincerely kind. The less evolved part of me wished he had been a brat.

It was obvious that Mase was surprised to see me. Bella did not play her hand and walked right up to the bleachers, climbing three rows right to us.

"Hey, Lanie," she said, reaching for my hand and smiling widely. "It is so nice to see you again."

Rather than make a scene, of which I was tempted but would never do in in public, I simply pulled my hand away and turned my back, ignoring her completely.

Lisa and I made small talk until they took the hint and turned to climb down the bleachers. Mase had a deer in the headlights look on his face, muttered something about how good it was to see me before holding out his arm for her as she descended row by row. He looked small and unsure as I watched him out of my periphery amble along behind Bella towards the bleachers on the other side of the gym, where he and his…whatever she was…sat down behind the opposing team's bench. Occasionally when I randomly glanced at them— making sure never to be caught staring— she would kiss him on the cheek or have her hand on the inside of his thigh, and this last gesture is what did it. I'm not sure why, except for the intimate nature of her touch and that she did it in public, in front of me, his wife, and everyone else.

****

"Thanks for texting," he said nervously. "There's so much I want to say to you, and I didn't know if I'd get the chance."

I'd been ignoring his calls and texts since he left and now that he was here in front of me, I could see what Lisa had been trying to tell me. He looked pitiful, like he had lost at least ten pounds.

"As you can imagine, this has been awful for me. And Z." I sounded cold and distant, more so than I intended.

"I can't tell you how sorry I am," he said, "and I know sorry isn't enough, but I can't find the words to express how much I regret what I did."

He looked tired, like he hadn't slept, but he was wearing the aqua fishing shirt I gave him on his last birthday that I really loved, and I thought that took intention on his part. I suddenly felt compassion for him.

"Listen, the reason I texted is because we have some things to discuss that concern our son." We had been separated for a couple months and my due date wasn't far off. Texting him wasn't necessary, but I missed him so much and wanted to see him without being vulnerable and I thought this was a plausible reason for us to talk. It was the first time since I asked him—told him—to leave.

"Oh my God," he said, dropping his head into his hands, "I thought you were going to ask me for a divorce." He wiped his face with his sleeve and took a seat on the porch swing where we'd sat together so many times discussing our lives, our plans for the future, everything. Times I missed. I sat on the rocker quietly while he continued.

"Listen, Lane, I don't know how to go forward, or if that is even what you want," he took a deep breath "but I love you and I want our family back," he added firmly, looking straight ahead not at me.

I was glad to hear that–he wanted *our* family, but I was still too angry to take him back and I wasn't sure if I would ever fully trust him again.

"Well, I guess you should've thought about that before you decided to give Bella such a warm welcome home."

He looked wounded by my sarcasm, and I regretted the words as soon as I said them. I didn't want to hurt him—I just couldn't seem to control the words as they poured from my mouth with the force of Niagara Falls. I didn't even take a breath between sentences.

"You all look like quite the happy family in public. No wonder everyone thinks you've reconciled with her."

He didn't say anything for a few minutes, but then stood up and stepped toward me. He took my hands in his.

"Lanie, I understand you're angry, but I hope in time you will forgive me. Bella and I are not together as a couple, we do things together for West. You know I love you and if you let me, I will spend the rest of my life proving to you and Z that I am the man you know deep down I am."

****

Birthday parties at the club were over the top and spared no expense. I shouldn't have been surprised that this is where they, Olivia and Bella, would have West's birthday party. They were thick as thieves. Lisa was invited because AJ was invited, and although he was at the age where he could have been dropped off and then picked up after the party ended, Leese chose to stay.

"I wouldn't miss this show for anything," she said.

I was invited under the pretext of being West's stepmother—a term I despised—and I'm sure to allow Bella to rub in that she slept with my husband, but I wasn't going to let her win. Mase had asked me to go with him as a show of his commitment to me and I agreed, after his relentless persistence, to give him a chance, much to Lisa and Zoey's happy support, but with no guarantees for a future.

The activities took place between the Olympic style pool, which was flanked on one side with regulation clay tennis courts and on the other with an outdoor grill/restaurant and game room, and the stables that housed prize winning horses used for riding lessons, under a large tent with the sides rolled up. It was cooler this time of year, the break between Thanksgiving and Christmas, and an excellent time for outdoor activities and parties.

Mase held my hand as we walked through the main Club building and then outside under the huge covered outdoor lounge. It was like a maze with its 50 large TV screens positioned at every angle possible, toward a quiet, stone path that led through some of the old, large Cypress trees dotting the landscape and out into the venue. It was a lovely, canopied walkway that was quiet except for the sounds of the squirrels scampering about. Mase stopped unexpectedly and kissed me.

"I love you," he said.

He stepped back and smiled that sexy smile I fell in love with, took my hand deliberately, and we made our way to the gift table under the large white party tent.

West was standing next to a picnic table piled high with gifts and perusing his cache as I handed him his present. It was easily identifiable, a new 12 gauge shot gun in a case, but I wrapped it anyway.

"Oh man, thanks Lanie," he said, beaming. "You too, Dad."

I still wasn't comfortable hearing this little boy refer to my husband as dad, but I didn't flinch and that was progress. He was also calling me "Lanie" now instead of Miss Lanie, despite Bella's insistence on the formal. It made me feel a bit closer to him.

Bella appeared surprised to see me, or more accurately, me and Mase together, I think. But I was there for West, because he was a sweet kid, and more importantly, to me anyway, I was going to make a statement, literally, to her. Watching her buzz around savoring her role as my husband's son's mother infuriated me. It wouldn't have bothered me quite as much if she hadn't slept with him recently, but her plan was obvious, at least to me and Leese. The rage I had toward her was something I had never felt before—not in this way—it was difficult to articulate, and it simmered just below the surface. I promised myself I would try not to make a scene, given it was West's birthday party. In a tender conversation on the drive over, Mase said I should do or say whatever I felt like I needed to do or say to her, not in a give me permission way, but in a supportive, you have every right to do what you want, and I am on your side, way. Then he apologized again.

Mental Note: I love him and I know he loves me. I can feel it. I think I might be able to move past his mistake. I hope I can.

Olivia was sitting at a round table in the center of the tent area, and not surprisingly, her minions were close by. She raised her eyebrows a bit when she saw us—an inexperienced observer would have missed it. We followed protocol and in between greeting other parents, navigated our way to her.

After Mase's standard greeting, "Mother," Olivia looked me over and said, "Well, dear, you look fine considering everything."

I held my tongue because Olivia was now a secondary character to me.

The children were riding four-wheelers and shooting skeet and generally running amuck with fun. There were archery targets set up, and dirt trails where children disappeared into dense woods before reappearing to the east of the golf course. They moved together, the pre-teen boys, in a pack from one location to another. You would have thought it was a birthday party for a prince. And maybe it was, but Mase surely didn't act that way.

"Hey, Lanie," Bella said, as she walked by me with a tray of cupcakes, acting like she was simply a hostess and hadn't slept with my man.

I saw this as my opportunity, and I immediately

jumped on it. I'd thought for a while about what I would say to her, but in the moment I just said what I felt about her, my man and life in general.

"Look," I said, smiling while I took the tray from her and randomly passed out cupcakes to dirty grabbing hands. "It's over. Mase and I and our children are a family no matter what you do—so you can just pack up and take your whore self back to wherever you came from, or you can camp out with Olivia, it doesn't matter. It's over. You lost."

I handed a chocolate iced delight to a freckled, breathless boy and smiled at him. I felt empowered, like I was taking back control of my life. Bella seemed surprised that I confronted her, and yet she too, kept on like nothing was wrong.

"Call me whatever you like," she responded as she leaned down to pick up a random cupcake wrapper that had been tossed on the ground. "But it isn't over," she said, "not by a long shot."

I probably shouldn't have been surprised by that, but I was. I guess I hoped she would accept Mase's decision and move on, or ideally, move away.

"Don't count on it, honey," I said, as confidently as I could. "Do your best, but it'll never be enough."

When I finished speaking, I handed her the tray and left her standing alone, speechless.

****

"I heard him tell them both," Leese said, "when he was helping them load that monstrous tank Bella drives with West's presents."

Lisa was responding to my retelling of the brief interaction I'd had with Bella with some info of her own.

She put her feet up on the dash and took a sip of

water. She and I were driving home from the party together. Mase was bringing West and AJ with him.

"Interesting," I said, curious to know more. I took the water bottle out of her hand and took a sip. "And?"

"And well, he said that he loved you and that he was going to make it work with you no matter what he had to do. Bella didn't say much, but Olivia told him he was making a mistake and Mase told her to shut up," she said, grinning.

"He told her to shut up?"

"He did," she said, and then I thought that maybe we might be okay.

Chapter 14

The contractions came unexpectedly, fast and hard. Our son wasn't due for another couple of weeks, but he was ready and we barely made it to the hospital. His entrance was quick and uncomplicated—three pushes and he was here. I was relieved and glad Mase was with me.

Within an hour after my water broke, he was joyfully introducing our son to the collective gathered outside my hospital door.

"Lord," Leese said as she squeezed past the crowd and into my room, "you'd think Dale Jr or Nick Saban was signing autographs out there."

I smiled and nodded in agreement.

"Where's Z?" Lisa asked.

"She went to get me some pizza," I said, smiling broadly.

"Ah, yes, the post-delivery craving." More softly she said, "Feeling okay?"

"Yeah, a bit tired and sore, but he was quick, thank God."

Just then Mase's phone dinged with a text.

"Hey, check that, will you, please? It's been going off non-stop."

Leese grabbed the phone as Z popped back in with our favorite thick crust extravaganza.

"Damn, you'd think Dale Jr was out there," she said,

as she opened the pizza box and lifted out a stringy, gooey piece and handed it to me.

Childbirth was almost worth it if this was the reward.

Lisa excused herself and stepped out of the room, leaving me and my daughter a chance to talk privately.

"How are you, hon?" I asked, wiping sauce from my chin.

"I'm good, Mom. You're the one who just had a baby."

"Yes, I know, I'm just checking."

She'd been stressed because the months were passing and RJ's graduation was in May and then he'd be off to Florida State.

"It's all good. We've got a ten-year plan."

I should have known. Zoey was always a planner and honestly the most organized person I knew.

Chapter 15

It was December. Christmas time, and Banjoland was bustling with activity. The nostalgia of Christmases past with my people and the wonderful memories of Mase going out of his way to make sure Z and I were happy and warm and cozy created many happy times for us.

Ad was coming home for the holidays, as Congress was taking its winter break, and Leese was preparing for the big Christmas bash they put on each year for the locals. Hunting was in full swing. RJ came by early this morning to pick up Z so that they could get in a deer stand and he could "provide" before their day required structure. I applauded her willingness to forgo sleep to sit in a deer stand with her man, but I settled for pics she sent me from her phone rather than a personal experience.

****

The Christmas bash was one of my favorite activities each year. And because it grew year after year with a more eclectic group of people, and because having wait staff and those to prepare food made it much easier on those of us who did all that in the beginning, Ad and Lisa moved it to the club. One of the best things, in my opinion, was that we could invite anyone we wanted— you didn't have to be a Club member to attend because it was a private party. It was the one time of year that the

Banjolanders dressed up, mostly without complaint, as the food and beer were free, and that alone put people in a festive mood. I was particularly looking forward to this party because it was the last big event before the fishing season began in a few months. All seasons in Banjoland were described by the type of hunting or fishing that occurred during those months. It was also a chance to show off the baby, which was Mase's idea, and Zoey agreed to take him home after a little while because she didn't like how the party had evolved into a "pretentious, fake, 'look at me'" event anyway.

We approached the entrance to the Club as always, and Simon helped me get out of the truck and unhook Clark's car seat carrier contraption. Mase grabbed the oversize Gucci diaper bag that Lisa brought back for us on her last trip to DC, took my hand from Simon's and led me to the long wooden bench on the terrace outside the entrance.

"Here you go, man," he said, tossing Simon the keys along with a green and red monogrammed envelope. "Merry Christmas. We appreciate you."

Mase was always good about the details.

"Thank you, sir, thank you very much." His smile was radiant and took off to park the truck.

"That was sweet," I said to Mase.

"Well, that's just who I am," he joked. "Come here and sit for a minute. I have something for you."

We sat together for a moment while he foraged through his jacket pocket. It was dark, but colorful Christmas lights softly glowed, intertwined with greenery along the windows and entryway. Two large fir wreaths adorned with silver ornaments and red ribbon were centered on each massive door. Christmas music softly piped overhead. I was relaxed and healing.

"I thought we agreed not to give each other gifts this year, with the baby and all," I said, but pleased that he knew me well enough to know that I was always open to receiving gifts.

"I know, I know. I had this made specially and I just couldn't wait to give it to you."

He presented a small black, velvet pouch with the words "Cartier" across the middle. My excitement grew as I pulled apart the drawstring and let the shiny gold band fall into my palm. It was a yellow gold band, with what looked like a two-carat diamond in the middle and flanked by a smaller diamond on each side.

"The middle diamond represents us, and the others are for Z and Clark," he said.

I smiled widely as admired the ring.

"I want you to know that you're the love of my life," he said, "and I will spend the rest of my life proving it you. I love you with all of me."

We kissed tenderly and I was overcome with love for him.

****

The party was in full swing when we entered, and our friends were obviously enjoying themselves. The band was playing jazzy versions of Christmas carols, waiters were mingling with hors d'oeuvre trays held over their heads, and champagne was flowing freely.

Lisa waved for us to come join her and Ad at their table. She looked beautiful in a gold mini that showed off her athletic and tanned legs.

"What took you so long?"

I held out my hand for her to inspect the reason for my tardiness.

"Nice! You deserve it, too," she said, giving it the once over. "But listen, I have news."

She took the baby out of his carrier and held him across her chest.

Before she could tell me, Bella appeared in a figure flattering red number, with short, capped sleeves and a low v-neck exposing her perfect cleavage. The stilettos added to her sexy presentation. She looked fantastic. The room paused for a moment before everyone resumed their conversation and she made her way to Olivia's table. That was the only drawback of having the Christmas party at the Club—members were allowed, and that meant Olivia would be right in the middle of everything.

"Focus," Lisa said and turned my head with her hand so we were face to face.

"What? What do you know?"

"Ad said that he heard through some back channels in Washingtonthat Senator Downes has something big in the works."

"Well, that isn't really surprising, is it?"

"Oh, and there's this," she said and after scrolling for a minute, handed me her phone.

It was a picture of Senator Downes at a restaurant with a cute young woman and if you enlarged the picture you could see his hand on her thigh under the table.

"Ewe," I said, "but not surprising. Where did you get this?"

"Ad said there's all kinds of information available for sale to an interested buyer. He thought we might need something like this one day. It's not a big deal on its own, because obviously everyone knows he cheats, but he's lacking discretion, and this could be helpful to us one day in combination with something else, you know, for down the road."

Ad approached the table and sat down next to me.

"Missed you." I gave him a large hug. "Thanks for getting info on the senator."

"Anytime," he said, squeezing me tight. Leaning back, he looked me over and said, "You look really good."

"Keep him, Leese," I pronounced in response to his compliment, but she wasn't paying attention.

I followed her eyes across the room to Bella and Mase sitting at the bar laughing at something West was saying. It looked like he was telling them a story while waving his arms and doing a little dance.

After a couple of minutes, the bartender gave Mase two drinks and he stood up, said something to them and began walking toward our table. As he approached, he could tell by the look on my face that I didn't like the scene I'd just observed.

"So sorry, Lane, I ordered drinks and they came up to talk with me while I waited," he said, and then kissed me and looked me in the eyes. "You're the only one for me."

This journey was going to be more difficult than I thought.

Mase took our son from Lisa, who had become unusually quiet, and he and Ad began circulating through the crowd showing off the baby and becoming engulfed in the jovial atmosphere.

"That bitch," Lisa said.

"Well, yes, but he is going to have to interact with her because of West, and I don't want it to be difficult for Mase to have a relationship with him. And remember, *he* is just as guilty as she is."

"She's a snake," Lisa snipped, "and she needs to go."

I agreed and together we drank and schemed conspiratorial scenarios for Bella's demise until we left the party and gathered again at our place.

****

RJ and Z and a group of their friends left the party ahead of us and were on the patio next to the covered porch playing life-sized Jenga. Mase had built a firepit on the patio and Z and her friends often hung out there on the weekends. Tonight, it was the regulars involved in games and karaoke.

I took Clark into the house and put him to bed. He was just a little less than a month old, but he was sleeping through the night and for that I was quite thankful.

I changed into shorts and a sweatshirt and joined everyone, most still dressed for the party, on the patio. It was cool, but the firepit gave off a lot of heat.

Ad and Mase were observing the game and debating strategy as Greggins pulled the wrong piece of wood that sent the entire structure crumbling to the ground, to applause by Z and RJ and laughter from Carrie Ann, his girlfriend.

"So, Mel," Lisa said as we rocked on our chairs enjoying the vibe, "I need to fill you in."

Her silhouette, framed by the fire that gave her an orange glow, made her look oddly unearthly as she continued.

"Remember the night when Clark was born and Mase kept getting texts and you told me to look at his phone and then I stepped out as Z came in"?

The familiar feeling I associated with Bella washed

over me.

"It was her, wasn't it?"

"It was, but the messages weren't overt. They mostly said she's heard the baby was born and she'd like to meet him next time he came by to get West."

"Please tell me you scrolled through his texts."

"Duh," she said, rolling her eyes.

The fact that I was even concerned about what was in the texts made me angry at Mase. I tried to keep things in perspective and not bring up his whatever it was with her…one night stand—to put it nicely—and to try and move forward and forgive him. Sometimes I handled it well, and sometimes not so well. But he was always patient and kind with me, even when I unexpectedly raged at him.

I held my breath and waited.

"She invites him over a lot, usually under the guise of seeing West, but there's always a little innuendo there. It is like she's tossing out a line to see if he will bite. But he always rejects nicely," Leese said.

"Bitch," we said in unison.

"He told me I could read his texts and scroll through his phone, I just haven't. I wish she would just disappear."

Chapter 16

Graduation had been looming over this year for Zoey. Knowing her guy was going off to college while she had two more years in high school suddenly became real.

She had gone to all his senior year events; homecoming, sports banquet, prom, and was planning on following him to State once she graduated. Their life together was planned, and even though I thought she was too young to have her life planned out as a 10th grader— that she needed to travel and meet other people and experience more of life—she had always been an old soul and somehow it seemed like it would be okay.

The graduation ceremony was held at the local Baptist church where pastor Waylon Earl had been preaching for forty years. It was common for a graduation in the South to be held at a church and this ceremony would be followed by a community picnic on the expansive lawn that surrounded the 150-year-old clapboard structure. I was looking forward to relaxing under the ginormous live oaks with family and friends and celebrating this moment that included lots of homemade food.

We took our seats toward the back of the church, which for some reason was our customary place to sit when in a church. The entire town seemed to be present, as it was one of the traditional yearly gathering opportunities. Mary Sue was accompanied by her sister and other family members and as she made her way to her reserved seat in the front of the church, she stopped to chat with many of the people who impacted RJ's life. As she passed our pew, she gave both Mase and me a long hug and took Zoey's hand so she would follow her down the aisle and sit with Mary Sue and her family, which was fine with me.

The graduates were beginning to line up outside the church as Aideen pushed through the crowd. She waved to us as she entered, hoping we would have room for her in our pew, which of course we did. Aideen had been around our kids so much, not only as a housekeeper, but as Greggins' mother, she was like a surrogate parent to all of them.

"It's a zoo out there," she said, squeezing by me and plopping down on the only vacant spot in our pew.

"I know," I said. "I can't believe they're graduating. Time flies."

Mase interrupted our chat by gently elbowing me and pointing to a page in the commencement program he was reading.

"Look," he said.

I took the booklet and followed his finger. I have to say I was surprised. Even after everything that happened, he was still a power player in this community.

"Wow," I said, "whose decision was this anyway?"

"I'm not sure," Mase said, but we were both equally surprised that Senator Downes was listed as the keynote speaker. It didn't make any sense to me. Maybe 2nd National Bank was funding a school addition, or a new field house, or something of substance. Who knows? It was obvious he was not going to fade out of sight, that is for sure.

His speech was like every other graduation speech that I'd heard, and likely the same as every other speech happening on this day, and probably plagiarized. He droned along until his final sentence, which put everything into perspective.

"And in closing, not only do I wish these graduates the best of luck as they look to the future, but I would also like to announce that I am officially running for my former congressional seat in Washington, to get back to work on the things that matter to all of us."

Mase and I looked at each other and grimaced, and his look was so goofy I almost laughed out loud.

As Principal Bobby Brock began announcing each senior's name, I quietly texted Leese. "Senator Downes just announced he is running for his old senate seat. WTH?"

Her reply was immediate.

"Yes – just heard. WTH?"

As hats were tossed in the air, and congratulations proliferated through the masses, we hurried out ahead of everyone so we could process together this extraordinary news. We strolled across the lawn and through the sea of parked cars to Mase's truck, where we gathered our cooler full of goodies and traditional picnic lunch, complete with Mimosas.

"Can you believe that?" I said, almost rhetorically.

"He hijacked the graduation ceremony for his own purpose, but that's not surprising," said Mase. "Still, as a convicted felon, can he legally run for the Senate?"

"I don't know, but I imagine he would've checked on everything before deciding to run."

At least I would think so. I also thought about Ad

and was glad that he was a congressman so they wouldn't be running against each other.

As Mase opened the plaid blanket and spread it evenly under a small group of oaks, the citizenry of Banjoland mingled and laughed and it reminded me of what I thought a church social would be like in the 1800s, on a grander scale. It was sunny, but not too hot, and the trees provided ample shade. Buddy Brock was making his rounds, making sure each family knew how special their graduate was and how his or her future was bright and almost any other platitude you can think of. He acted like someone running for office, and after considering this for a moment, I realized that was, in fact, what he was doing. In Banjoland, especially in local situations, the few in power can make decisions and take actions according to what they think, and those actions don't necessarily have to be fact based. Buddy had come close to being ousted a few years back because of some rumors about him and a female student. I'm not sure if there was truth to any of it, but nevertheless, there was a call for his ouster and he had barely hung on to his job.

At that moment, RJ, Z, Greggins and Carrie Ann showed up, plopped on the blanket and began rummaging through the various containers of food like they were refugees.

"Easy," I said, and handed them plates.

"Greg, where's your mom?" I wanted to make sure she knew to join us, and I forgot to mention it to her while we were in the church.

"She's around here somewhere," he said and scanned the sea of people on the lawn looking for her.

"There she is." He pointed toward the church steps, where we saw her in deep conversation with Senator

Downes. It wasn't surprising that she would be chatting with him; she had worked for him and Olivia for many years. What was odd was that he would take the time, in public, to talk with her, as his mode of operation was to be seen with high-profile individuals or those who could advance his agenda.

The consummate gentleman, Mase went to retrieve her so she could join us, which required him to have obligatory conversation with his father. As he wandered toward them, mimosa in hand, he chatted with just about everyone along the way. I admired his people skills and that he genuinely cared about others. I also admired his genuine kindness, but at this moment I simply found him hot. He was tan and his hair was a bit longer than normal, which gave it a little curl, and his body was toned and muscular.

Sue Ellen saw my gawking, as she called it.

"Looks good, girl," she said.

"I know. Doesn't he?"

Billy interrupted by pulling up his shirtsleeves and posing his arms, so his biceps, what there was of them, could show.

"I know I look good," he cracked. "You know you want some of this."

"That's right, baby," Sue Ellen said. "You're the man." She handed him a covertly poured beer into a Dale Junior plastic cup.

Our joviality was interrupted by successive dings, so we knew someone was getting texts.

"Not me," Mary Sue said. "I'm still off from the ceremony."

We all looked at our phones, but no one had any texts.

"Hang on, "I said, "Mase left his phone. Look, it's under the corner of the blanket."

I picked up his phone and saw three text messages and wondered who would text him on a Saturday when everyone in Banjoland was here.

I punched in his passcode—Zoey's birthday—and hit the text icon. They were from her and she was wearing lingerie. The first one was a selfie and said, "miss this?" I tapped the second message. It was another selfie of her in lingerie that said, "miss you." The last one was a picture of her and West that said, "come see us, your family misses you."

I took a deep breath but it didn't help as my heart rate sped up and my temperature rose.

"What is it?" Sue Ellen asked.

"Nothing," I said, "just something stupid."

I immediately, as a knee jerk reaction, forwarded the texts to Leese. She was set to return from DC tomorrow.

Again, she immediately replied to my phone.

—You haven't said anything to him yet, have you?—

I responded.

—No.—

—Don't. I'll be home tomorrow, and we'll figure out what do about this whole situation.—

We both knew it would be almost impossible for me not to say anything.

A minute or so went by and my phone rang.

"I know," I said before she could utter a word.

"Look," she said in that tone let me know she was serious, "listen to me. You have to handle this thing correctly and flying off the handle with him is probably not the best way to deal with it. Please," she implored, "please wait until I get home tomorrow to talk about it and make a plan. Please."

"Okay," I said, half-heartedly, "I'll try."

I knew Lisa was right, but I was so angry at Bella, and then at Mase for creating this situation, but I knew I should listen to her. I needed to remain calm and create a thoughtful approach to deal with this rather than let my anger guide my decisions.

I clicked end and looked up to find Aideen and Mase making a Mimosa.

"Guess what?" Mase said, pouring too much champagne in the glass and licking the side while it overflowed.

"What?"

"My father is interested in having Greg work on his campaign and then when he's elected, working in his office."

Greggins was only fourteen years old, but even at this age had a reputation throughout the county as a hard working honest boy.

"What?" I was momentarily distracted by this news.

"Yes," he said, more relating information than opining about it.

Aideen jumped in. "Isn't it great?" she said happily, swallowing her drink in one gulp.

"Sure," I said. "Sure is."

****

Lisa came over like she said she would as soon as she got home and got AJ settled after his stay with a buddy while they were out of town.

"Okay," she said as I handed her some champagne, "I've been giving this some thought and I have some ideas."

"I have some ideas, too," I said derisively.

"Mase hasn't mentioned these texts to you, right?"

"Right."

"And you've looked through all of them, right?"

"Right."

"And you don't think he's involved with her other than for West, right?"

"Right. He's said before that eventually she'll get the message that he's not interested, but he wants to be careful so he can still have a relationship with West."

"Well, then," she said, "maybe it's time to involve the court. There are rules about visitation." She went on to explain how that might work in our favor.

I decided that I would hold my tongue until I couldn't anymore and then follow Lisa's suggestions.

Chapter 17

Summers in Banjoland were sweltering, and no matter how many I'd been through, I was always surprised at how hot it got. It always gave me flashbacks to our entrance into Clarksville and the heat radiating off the pavement. Early mornings were cool though, if cool meant 75 degrees, but compared to the stifling humidity of mid-afternoon temperatures that were over 100 degrees, it was a relatively cold spell.

The 4th of July was the next annual gathering, and it took place at Clark's Creek. Aside from the oppressive heat, which I will say that you never get used to but can grow to tolerate, it is a fun time of drinking and fellowship. It was also the last bash we would have before RJ left for Florida State for good. He had made periodic trips back and forth to set up his dorm and to attend orientation and some football training camps, but soon he would be gone until Thanksgiving. In his honor, I made cupcakes with his jersey number, as State was going to let him walk on and try out for the football team. This was a huge conversation among the Banjoland men, as they felt it was their responsibility to Ray's memory to make sure things went as smoothly as they could for RJ, and that he made good decisions. I also surprised him and Z with tickets to a Broadway show they had expressed interest in attending. I did this on the down low because the Banjoland men would have harassed him excessively if they knew of his affinity for musical theater, but it just made me love him more.

The events of the day started early, with everyone meeting at the creek around 6:00am to take canoes on the water to the party cabin. I can't express how happy I was when I found out a few years back that they were building a cabin on Billy Joe's creek property that we could use for these occasions. It meant indoor plumbing and air conditioning, and that's what made it bearable for me. Plus, this was Clark's first time on this adventure, and he would need nap time and cool air. At first I didn't want to bring him because honestly it was a drunk fest in the heat. But after discussion with Mase and a realization that all children in Banjoland participate in this event no matter their age, and that not everyone got drunk—it was usually the same culprits—I decided to give it the old college try.

It was a fabulous weather day, cooler morning air, sun shining and happy people when we gathered at the livery to get our canoes. Z and RJ and Greggins and Carrie got theirs first and had some contraption RJ created that held their two canoes together. Ad and Leese and Mase and I loaded up our children. West got in with Lisa and Ad so he could hang out with AJ, and we had the baby and all of his accouterments.

West often hung out with us, especially when AJ was around, and the more I got to know him the more I liked him. What I didn't like was Bella using him to keep constant tabs on Mase and what was happening with our family. I did my best to keep my thoughts in check, but I was vigilant and never let my guard down. Mase's contact with her seemed appropriate, but I was always watching and listening.

We began paddling toward the cabin and after a mile or so pulled onto a sandbar so the children could swim and jump off the rope swing that hung from a massive live oak. I was relaxed, sitting on a cooler and feeding Clark when I saw them pull up a few feet in front of the sandbar.

"Hey y'all," she said, sporting a pair of cutoff jean shorts and a red bikini top.

I didn't recognize the man with her.

"Hey, Bella," someone swimming yelled.

"Hey, Mom." West swam over to her canoe.

Before I could ask, Mase leaned down and whispered, "I have no idea why she's here."

I had an idea.

I'd been trying, hard, to not make waves and to do my best to get along, but there was no way we were going to start socializing with her.

"You okay?" he asked.

"Of course. Go swim with the guys," I encouraged. He kissed me for a longer than normal time, then body slammed himself into the water, drenching those around him.

Lisa swam up and toweled off before taking a seat on the cooler next to me.

"What the hell?" she said.

"I don't know. Who is the guy?"

"Ad says he works for Senator Downes at the bank."
Figures.

I could endure the rest of the trip as long as she didn't come close.

"Hey Lisa, Lanie," Bella said as she exited her canoe and proceeded towards us, new guy trailing close behind. "This is my friend Todd. He works at 2nd National." She dragged over a random cooler and sat next to us like she was part of the group—like a friend.

We smiled at Todd and he continued walking toward a group of guys who were standing under a tree in the water and drinking beer – oddly acceptable in the morning on these trips.

Lisa did not hold back.

"What are you doing here?" she quizzed.

"I was invited and my son is here," she answered like she'd expected the question.

Lisa didn't give me a chance to say anything.

"You're not welcome here," she said. "You're not our friend and you need to leave."

Bella responded without hesitation. "Our son is here and whether or not you like it, I will go where I choose." And looking directly at me, she said, "It's not my problem if you can't keep your man happy at home."

All my good intentions evaporated, and I impulsively pushed her off the cooler.

"You're nothing but a whore," I said while she scrambled to compose herself.

She looked startled but kept her poise as she calmly regained her footing and brushed the sand from her shorts. Without further comment she strolled over to Todd, speaking to people along the way—most wondering, like us, why she was there in the first place, but too mannerly to ask.

After thirty minutes or so, we resumed our pilgrimage towards the cabin—with no sign of Bella and Todd.

"I told them I thought it was best they leave," Mase said, "so they turned at the pump house and circled back to the livery."

My mood immediately lightened.

"How did she take that?" I asked.

"Said whatever I thought was best."

He took Clark from my arms and headed for the cabin to put him down for his nap. I relaxed on a tire shaped inner tube while Lees and I discussed my next move.

****

She obviously wasn't expecting it and that was unfortunate because it could've been completely avoided. Bella's presence had become more invasive in our lives, and she had begun to use Mase's time with West overtly as a bargaining chip. After she crashed the canoe trip, she started making West's visits with Mase contingent on whether she could be part of them. Mase was gentlemanly with her, but her façade of easing West into their relationship was no longer valid and, at this point, completely unnecessary. She still presented herself differently to Mase than she did to me, but she seemed more desperate in her efforts to spend time with him.

It was his idea because of how Bella had been acting, and because of financial obligations he would have regarding West in the future, that he legally secure his rights and responsibilities toward his oldest son. That way she couldn't really control their visits and because of his age, it wasn't necessary that she be overinvolved. I was surprised and relieved but held that in and instead asked him how she responded to his suggestion.

"I don't understand why you want to do this," she'd said, once Mase decided to move forward with this action. "It's not necessary—I trust you to do what's right." She was almost pleading, he said, and it seemed odd.

Part of the process, our lawyer said, was to legally establish paternity and then file paperwork with the court establishing Mase's rights and responsibilities. I thought that was an excellent idea, not because Mase wouldn't be responsible, but that there would be clear guidelines as to what Bella could do and what she couldn't do, and in my opinion, eliminate much of her manipulative power.

Chapter 18

RJ had settled in at State, and Z was confident that their relationship would survive this new arrangement. Today we were going to take over a few odds and ends he requested from Mary Sue's because he had a free day from pledging a fraternity with a few other football players who were going to help. I had mixed feelings about Greek life and the time it might take away from his studies and football, but I supported him and so did Z.

Before we did anything, Mase and I did what we always did on Saturday mornings. Even after everything, we still connected instinctively and passionately at this level. It took a while for me to be able to physically love him after I found out his affair with Bella, and he was patient while I told him how disgusted it made me to even look at him naked. Thinking back, I sometimes wonder if I had been too harsh with him, but then immediately discount that and try not to think about it too much. I was healing, but certainly not there yet.

Mase snuggled into my back and I could immediately feel he was ready.

"I just woke up." I yawned.

"But I've been awake and waiting for you," he whispered.

He slowly ran his hands down my back and down my leg. I turned on my back and he tenderly began massaging my breasts. I was beginning to become aroused and I arched a little as he traced his fingers over my tight abs until they found their home between my legs. He had me squirming within a minute and I rolled him over and gave him an oral morning greeting. His moans were too much for me and I thought I was going to orgasm before I even mounted him, but I managed to use some brief self-control as I slid over his body and lowered myself onto him, squeezing (thanks to diligent Kegel exercises) with every stroke and his moans escalated until I couldn't take it anymore and we orgasmed intensely before I collapsed on him.

"Happy Saturday, my love," he said while stroking my hair.

"Same to you, sexy," I said, and added, "but next time let me brush my teeth so we can kiss."

"Whatever you say," he laughed.

"Hey, break it up in there," Z bellowed through the door. "We've got things to do and places to go."

"Give us a minute," I said, fully knowing our intimate moment was over.

"You already had a minute," she said, "and at your age, that's all you should need."

****

He pulled up in the drive unannounced in his trademark white Dooley with the farm logo on the door as Mase was loading our truck with a mini-fridge and an old chest of drawers we were giving RJ.

I watched through the kitchen window while Clark's bottle was warming in the microwave. They shook hands and then the senator handed him a manila envelope. Mase opened it and flipped through the papers before returning them to the envelope and back to his father. The discussion became a little more intense and finally

Mase took the envelope, shook his father's hand and came back into the house.

"You're not going to believe this," he said.

I didn't think I could be surprised at this point.

I listened while Clark drank his brunch and Mase reviewed the documents in more detail.

"My father took it upon himself to have the family lawyer draw up the custody paperwork for West."

"How did he get involved?"

"I told him I was going to pursue establishing my rights legally where West was concerned, and he decided to ask Whit to do it for me."

"That was nice?" I offered.

"Well, from what I've read, it appears to be a more than fair and amenable agreement. It says I acknowledge I am West's father, and she acknowledges she is his mother. The visitation is very generous. It says we can share all the holidays, and she will let me decide. It gives us joint custody and it says we will split college costs. It says we will alternate weekends, unless we are doing something special, in which case she will adjust her weekends and weekdays are open for whatever West wants to do.

"What about child support?" I asked.

"Oddly, there's nothing in it about child support."

Mase had been paying for expenses and camps and other things for West but had not been contributing a set amount of money each month.

He continued, "It basically says that she can financially support him and that I can contribute what I think is necessary."

None of this made sense, I thought . How could she financially support him when she didn't have a job?

"None of this makes sense," Mase said. "It is too easy."

"What did your father say?"

"He said that it would be a good idea to keep our family business out of the courts and that he had spoken to Bella and convinced her it would be in her best interest to resolve this as civilly as possible, and she agreed. Then he said he had an appointment, handed me the papers and left."

We sat quietly while Clark finished his bottle and some squash, then Mase left the papers on the table and returned to his tasks outside.

****

"RJ is dropping out of State!" Z ranted as we finished loading the car. "He said thanks, but we don't need to bring any of this stuff to him because he is coming home."

"What? Why?" I asked compulsively. I mean technically he hadn't even started yet.

"Your father-in-law," she said sarcastically, "they had a meeting, and he offered RJ a job at the bank at an exorbitant salary and that Pops planned for RJ to move into politics and work with him once he wins the election. That he would help guide him and make him a huge success."

Mental Note: This is a very bad idea and I have a feeling there is a lot more going on here than the obvious.

"What does Mary Sue think?" I asked, taking a moment to process this turn of events.

"Oh, she's all in," Zoey said. "She thinks Pops is the greatest and will take care of RJ. I mean, what the hell?" she said, getting more irritated by the sentence. "I have planned my life around going to FSU to be with him. I am graduating early. I spent my entire summer interning in Washington, jumped through endless hoops to gain experience and get accepted into State's super competitive government relations program, and he made this decision without even talking to me. He just assumed I would support whatever he decided to do."

I don't remember her ever this angry. I didn't blame her, and I was surprised that RJ would make a decision like this without at least getting her input. He of all people should know better.

Mase interjected, "Come with me, honey, and let's talk."

He held out his hand, she took it and they walked together toward the barn and the back pasture.

This must have been why the senator went to meet Mary Sue, who was defensive when I called her to confirm all of this, and who anticipated my questions.

"Senator Downes said he had thought this through," she said, "and that he was certain it would be best for our family, and that he had a plan."

Adam had said those exact words to Lisa before their move to Banjoland.

I was careful not to be accusatory, even though I thought this was a ridiculous decision, that it was ridiculous for her to trust the senator and to allow her son to throw away his education on the word of a convicted felon who was likely responsible for her husband's death.

"I'm just wondering," I said, "by 'our' family, does that include Zoey?"

"Of course it does," she said, exasperated that I would suggest otherwise.

"I think she's concerned about his education and, from what I understand, he really didn't discuss this decision with her," I explained.

She said she never thought about that, but that Z should trust RJ to make the best decisions for them. I realized then that there was no changing her mind and shook my head in disappointment even though she couldn't see me from the other end of the phone and because in that moment it became clear to me just how unaware she really was about everything.

I hung up the phone, said a quick prayer for her and ventured off in search of Mase and Z. I found them leaning on a fence surrounding a small fishpond covered in duckweed.

"How's it going out here?" I asked and took a position on the fence between them.

"What do you think I should do, Mom?" Zoey asked, staring straight ahead.

"Well," I said, slowly and carefully choosing my words, "what do you want to do?"

"I want to go away to college like a normal person," she said. "We've been on a plan for a long time and now he wants to change everything. I am so aggravated I'm not sure what I'm going to do. No offense, Mom, but I am ready to leave home."

"None taken," I said, mulling over the potential outcomes of this news/these decisions.

The thought of her giving up her future to stay with RJ and ending up walking the path of politics scared me, especially because Senator Downes was driving this train. It is not overly dramatic to say that with one mistake he, or she, could end up dead.

This was a scary twist, but why, for what purpose?

Getting RJ to stay home didn't seem enough motivation or revenge for anything, but having a puppet that would execute his wishes would be a start. RJ loved Zoey, though, and must have realized that this would affect her, too. The question was how this would fit in with the senator's plan to get back at Mase (was that still a thing?), that Mase randomly reminded me was indeed still a thing.

Chapter 19

It was common knowledge that he was her regular side guy. Olivia certainly was no wallflower and had her share of paramours, which, I guess, is only fair if your husband is Senator Wes Downes. And although she had a variety of men over the years, she regularly kept company with Whittaker "Whit" Hughes, an attorney and retired banker (not surprisingly from the "other" bank in town, First Southern) and legacy of the largest landowners in Clarksville. He was a widower, handsome, traveled, and cultured. It was obvious they were regular companions, even dining publicly at the club under some flimsy guise that he was giving her financial advice, and oddly there were times the senator would join them. It was confusing to me, as I thought these sorts of affairs were supposed to be discreet and denied. Whit was completely smitten with her and didn't try to hide it. He was smart enough to see who she really was—and seemed to appreciate all the facets of the person that was Olivia Westhoven Downes.

Whit always liked me. We had some unspoken connection; I think part of it was that I reminded him of his estranged daughter. Since I first arrived in Banjoland he had done his best to offer guidance and education on the politics of Southern living, especially the group that I was thrust into when I became involved with Mase. His relationship with Olivia didn't impede ours at all, despite

106

her often and unmistakable attempts to sabotage us.

He also took a special liking to Z, always supporting and encouraging her adventures. That is why meeting him today for lunch was nothing out of the ordinary.

"You look lovely, as always," Whit said, standing from his seat at the corner window table, conveniently positioned away from the others, and pulled out my chair.

"Thanks," I said. "You're looking pretty dapper yourself."

One of the things I liked best about Whit was that he was completely pro Lanie when Mase had his fling. He ranted on about the injustice of it all and how Mase would never do better than me, and how he would live to regret his impulsive decision. He was loyal and for that he earned my permanent friendship.

We chatted pleasantly for a few minutes while we waited for our drinks. Once the waiter served my Mimosa and his gin and tonic, he left, not to return unless he got the nod from my companion.

Whit took a sip of his drink and lit a cigarette after offering me one, which I declined. He was unusually quiet, and it was then I realized there was a specific purpose for our meeting.

"Lanie, honey, I have something to tell you," he said, taking my hands in his.

What now?

"Don't be so dramatic," I joked, "just tell me."

He rubbed his chin with his thumb and forefinger and breathed deeply. "Okay, then," he said. And then he began.

When he finished, I was dumbfounded and speechless.

"Lanie…honey… are you OK?" he asked.

I didn't answer right away.

This is big.

"Are you sure?" I asked.

He nodded and took some papers from his jacket pocket and slid them across the table for me to peruse.

"Wow," was all I could say.

Knowing people who have connections can be a double-edged sword, as the saying goes. What was I supposed to do now?

Whit described how he attended a board meeting for the local community arts program at First National, when someone he didn't want to name asked him for a private meeting. He gave him the documents that Whit just let me see. It was a life insurance policy that Bella had on Senator Downes, which she kept in a safety deposit box at the bank. The policy listed her and her son West as the beneficiaries. It confirmed what Mase and I had suspected—that his father was supporting Bella and West, hence the need for the insurance, but the question remained as to why? Why would he have financed her return and continue to support her? Was he in on Olivia's plan to come between me and Mase? Was this part of his revenge? It did not really seem like his style and with each bit of new information I became more confused.

When Mase declined to sign the agreement that Whit drafted, which benefited Mase almost entirely, the senator was irate. It was almost an irrational anger. Mase tried to explain that he would rather go through the court and have things done in a legitimate and fair manner, so that it couldn't be perceived that he had used his family's influence or caused any type of duress, but that he appreciated the senator's effort. That was the last it was discussed.

"Thanks, Whit, but why are you showing this to me now?"

"You know I care about you, dear. I have since the day we met. I have overstepped as it is, but I need to tell you there is more. Keep reading."

I wondered what else there could be, so I kept reading until I came to the section that asked what the relationship was between the owner of the policy and the insured. It was unmistakable. Next to Mason Westhoven Downes III, the "insured" was "relationship to the purchaser." It clearly read "father of my child, Mason W. Downes V."

It took me a minute to grasp that this referred to the senator and not Mase.

"Whit," I whispered, making sure no one was within earshot. "Senator Downes is West's father?"

"It would appear that way." He methodically folded the papers and tucked them back into his jacket.

I had so many questions, and my thoughts were all over the place.

"I know this is a lot to take in all at once," Whit said, "but I think you can use this information to your advantage."

He was far ahead of me.

"Wait," I remembered, "what about the paternity test?"

He looked at me like my question/statement was ridiculous. He even rolled his eyes.

"Have you even seen the paternity test?"

We had not. Interestingly, the paperwork Senator Downes presented for Mase to sign didn't include having paternity test, and honestly, I don't think Mase ever questioned that he was West's father. And weirdly, neither had I. When he filed the traditional way, he admitted his paternity.

"Listen," he said, "I know this is a lot to take in all at once, but I think this can really help you take control of your situation. I have to ask you, however, not to reveal where you received this information."

I had so many questions. Why would the president of the bank give Whit this information? Why is Whit giving it to me? And does the fact that she listed her relationship like this even make it true? There was a lot of information to process and sort through, so I did what I would normally do in a situation like this.

"Whit…"

"Suffice it to say I have my own interests involved as well," he answered, and with that Olivia arrived and he promptly got up to greet her.

****

"Holy shit," Leese said, not one to normally cuss.

"I know," I answered reflexively.

We spent some time trying to figure it out. What could we do with this information if we couldn't say where it came from? And how could we prove whether it was true for sure, though we were both convinced it was without a doubt, true.

"Leese…"

"This changes everything," she said.

"I know."

We sat together on her porch swing while we tried to figure out what to do with this new information. It came to me suddenly and clearly. Leese was completely on board, as I expected she would be.

"What's with the intense conversation?" said Ad as

he breezed by us on his way to go turkey hunting with AJ. "Y'all look like you're plotting something."

He was home from congress for a long holiday weekend and was taking full advantage of the time he got to spend with his son.

"Look, Mom," AJ said, showing off the new shotgun he got for his birthday. He was careful not to point it at anyone and he treated it very respectfully. "I'm ready for a gobbler."

AJ had spent many hours in the woods with RJ and other local boys, and it popped into my head that West would likely be joining them on these adventures in the future.

"I'm sure you'll kill a big one," Leese added, "I can feel it. And I am sure Daddy will remember that size matters, right, Daddy?" She smiled warmly and winked at Ad, and they left discussing which deer stand they should hunt from and which way the wind was blowing.

"Now back to your idea," Leese said. "It's excellent."

****

"There must be a birth certificate," I said, while Whit finished off his martini. He signaled the waiter for another. I was glad he had agreed to meet me on such short notice.

"Indeed, there should."

I was mulling over how to begin the search, when he reached into his wallet, took out a card and slid it across the table to me.

J. Michael Phillips, Private Investigator
Private, Professional and Discreet.
Complete Satisfaction Guaranteed or your Money Back

"I have used him before," Whit said. "He is excellent."

I hadn't thought about using a private investigator.

"How much does he cost?" I asked, "and how long do you think it will take to find out something?"

"Just instruct him to send the bill to me," Whit offered. "I want to help you, Lanie honey. And I can't imagine it would take very long to find out something that should be on public record."

I didn't know what to say except thank you, so that is what I said repeatedly until he wouldn't hear it again. I knew that going forward, everything would change, but I didn't hesitate to make the call. I thought I was ready.

****

Lisa was completely on board with the private investigator plan and surmised that Whit had a harmless crush on me. I didn't think that was the case, as he was forty years older than I, but nevertheless I appreciated his generosity and always remembered to express that to him.

My meeting with J. (not Jay) was interesting and encouraging. He was sitting behind a desk that looked like it came off the set of the Andy Griffith show – big and heavy and oak. He stood when his secretary opened the door to let us in, revealing a short, but neatly groomed man and on the thinner side, wearing the kind of cowboy checkered shirt guys sported in the 1970s. He was mid-fifties I'd guess with a closely shaven beard and had a shaved head.

"Please have a seat." He pointed to the upholstered chairs in front of his desk.

He was very polite and took notes as we spoke. I gave him all the information I knew to give him, and he asked just a few questions.

"Your husband could simply have a paternity test, why aren't you pursuing that avenue?" he asked.

"I think he would need a reason and right now he doesn't think he has one. I want to get as many facts together as I can so he can make informed decisions," I answered.

"Okay, do you know where the child was born? What county?"

I didn't.

"Do you know if anyone witnessed the birth?"

I didn't.

"Do you know how the child was registered for school?"

I didn't.

I really didn't know anything.

"Okay," he said. "I will find out what I can and report back to you in a couple of days with any progress I have made. Frankly," he said, setting his pen on top of the pad, "this shouldn't be very difficult."

I was relieved. I didn't really want to play detective, and I had no idea how to go about finding information in a discreet way. The fact that Whit offered to pay for this was an unexpected bonus.

"Have you thought about what you will do with this information once it is confirmed?" Lisa asked me.

"Not completely," I said.

All I knew for sure was that I wanted to take the satisfaction away from Senator Downes by not allowing him to drop this bomb whenever he chose. It was obvious that Mase already loved West and that whoever shared this information was going to cause irreparable damage. At least I would be kind.

****

Everything happened so fast. It was hard to keep something this big from Mase, but I wanted to have all the facts before I told him anything, and I wasn't positive yet about how to do it.

I met with the investigator one week to the day after our initial meeting, at his office above a downtown coffee shop. I asked Whit to join me because I felt an obligation to him for his help to keep him in the loop. I agreed to meet Lisa immediately after we were finished.

I was nervous—like I imagined I would feel if I was waiting on the results of my own paternity test. Like when I was waiting for the results of the pregnancy test, knowing with one dark line my life would completely change. Whit and I arrived at the same time, and he escorted me through the lobby, up the stairs and into J's private office. J was on the phone and motioned for us to sit and we were silent as Whit pulled the chair back for me and we waited quietly for our host to finish his business.

"I'm glad y'all could make it," he said, ending his conversation and reaching into his desk to retrieve a folder. "As I mentioned during our initial meeting," he said, looking at me, "I didn't think this would take very long."

He handed me two documents he took from the folder.

"You'll see the first birth certificate has no father listed."

I reviewed it carefully. The space for the father's name was blank. I passed the paper to Whit.

"The second birth certificate, or the 'amended' certificate, filed three months later, does have a father's name added."

He handed me the key to my family's future.

My eyes focused immediately on the place for the father's name.

There it was, plain for all to see. West's father was indeed Mason Westhoven Downes III, according to this document. I didn't know how I should feel, but whatever I was feeling did not seem like it was how I should be feeling. I wasn't relieved. I was sad. Sad for Mase, sad for West. Just sad…and deep down, relieved.

"Here's an interesting fact that you need to know," J added. "For the child's school registration, for his entire life, as well as baseball registrations and everything else that requires a birth certificate, the one with the father's name missing has been used."

Whit said, "So what you are saying is that the child's mother has kept his paternity under wraps his entire life."

"It appears that way," J said. "Not only that, I had to dig deeply to find the second, amended certificate. It appears that this was intentional. The document is valid and legal, nonetheless."

"I don't know what to say, J, you've outdone yourself." Whit handed me back the documents.

"I really appreciate your help as well," I offered.

"Thanks, friend." Whit stood to shake his hand.

"One more thing before you leave," our private eye said.

We stood still while J handed me several pages of bank statements from the Downes Trust highlighting transfers to Bella. Substantial transfers.

Whit paid the bill, and after I thanked him profusely, I took myself and the documents straight to Lisa's house.

"I have been texting you for twenty minutes," she

said as I opened her front door. "What happened?"

I took the drink she presented and handed her the folder.

"Wow...that bitch," she said, after perusing the paperwork.

"Yeah."

"What are you going to do now?" she asked.

"I am not sure. I'm just not sure."

Chapter 20

As fall began in earnest, Banjoland came alive with the excitement of serious hunting and college football. RJ and Zoey were still a couple, but their relationship was strained as he began training for his position at the bank. The Senator was about to start seriously campaigning, and if he won, he promised both RJ and Greggins a position within his "organization." He sounded like the Godfather and RJ thrived on it, feeling like it could lead to opportunities down the road for him. Zoey began her Junior year of high school and, she said, was still planning on going to Florida State when she graduated.

I mulled over the information I received from Whit and J for a couple of weeks and decided I was going to confront Bella, since it seemed obvious to me that she was either blackmailing Senator Downes or they were on the same team with the same plan to wreck my relationship with my husband. I told myself I would give her the opportunity to set the record straight before I did, but I think I just wanted to see how she would respond. I wanted to be on the offensive and I wanted her to be uncomfortable. I wondered what she would say, and I wondered if Olivia knew the truth or if this is what Whit meant when he said he had his own interest in this situation.

I thought about confronting the senator, but he

scared me—something I never admitted to myself until I had to decide what to do with this explosive information. What if Olivia had no idea that he was West's father, and this is how she finds out? I also believed he was likely responsible for Ray's death, and certainly Sunglasses, though not likely to have done the actual deeds himself. And there were other deaths and disappearances that Mase said the senator was behind, and at the time I thought it was all so melodramatic, but over time and experience realized were likely true. And aside from all of that, this man was letting Mase raise his brother as his son! I was planning on telling Mase, that was always my plan, but I kept finding out new details and I wanted to have it all, and that included whatever reaction/information I got from Bella. That way I could present him with everything I knew. It didn't occur to me for a minute that this could be the wrong course of action.

I also thought about asking Leese to go with me, but she was completely unfiltered with Bella, and the situation would be challenging enough without pouring fuel on the fire. I vacillated between rage and disgust every time I saw her and now armed with these facts, I was ready to put her in her place, which I hoped eventually would be far from Clarksville.

"Okay," Leese relented. "I get it. But at least record her."

That was a great idea I had not considered.

****

"Well?" she said, as soon as I sat down across from her at Local's deli. "What is this big news I might find interesting?" She didn't make eye-contact and feigned nonchalance while she scrolled through phone

I wanted to slap her across her smug, make-up

covered face.

I was hoping to pique her interest so she would show up to meet me, and in that vein, I texted her and said I came across some information she might find very interesting. I was worried she would ignore me, but instead she responded almost immediately.

So much for pleasantries.

I asked for some water, declined food, and handed her a manila envelope with a copy of the amended birth certificate.

She glanced at the document but didn't react. She simply closed the folder, handed it back to me, and said, "So?"

I expected more. I don't know what, but more than this lack of reaction to what I thought was earth shaking information.

"So, since you and the senator have created this enormous lie that we are all living," I replied, calmy, "you need to be the one to tell him the truth."

She didn't blink an eye.

"No," she said, flatly. "This doesn't prove a thing. I'm not going to say anything, and neither are you."

"We'll see," I said, grabbing the folder and sliding my chair back to leave. She grabbed my arm as I brushed by her and whispered, "I'd think long and hard about what you do next," she warned. "The senator reacts badly when he feels threatened. Oh, and Melanie," she added as I snatched my arm from her grip, "I'm not going anywhere."

I left without further comment, evidence in hand, and made a beeline to Lisa.

****

"That bitch," she said after she heard the recording.

I was glad I remembered to have my phone already set to record when I entered the eatery.

"I know. Can you believe how arrogant she is?"

"What if we just confront the senator?" Leese offered.

We batted around some ideas, but I felt like it was time to just tell Mase the truth. I didn't want to hurt him, but obviously he needed to know and the sooner the better. I felt a little guilty for keeping it from him for this long, and now in retrospect I don't know why I thought Bella would just agree to suddenly be honest with him. I don't even know why I gave her the chance.

I told Leese she could share all of this with Ad once I told Mase this evening. I was nervous but determined and I hoped he would understand my actions but more my motive for holding this back for a while.

I took a shower, had a drink, and waited.

After an hour or so, I heard a truck door slam and I prepared myself as best I could to hurt the man I loved so deeply. I was surprised by a knock on the door, and I thought Mase had forgotten his key. I opened it to find my angry father-in-law towering over me. He grabbed me by the throat and slammed the door behind us.

"I'm telling you that you will never, *never*, tell my son what you think you know," he growled.

I could hardly breathe. I tried to pull his hands away from my neck, but he squeezed harder and I struggled to breathe.

"If you even think of opening that pretty little mouth of yours, you will regret it for the rest of your life, do you understand me?"

I nodded my head in agreement, silent tears streaking down my face.

"And for your silence, you will be well compensated. . . and so will Zoey. But speak one word to anyone and see what happens. Do not make that mistake."

He finished speaking, threw me across the room, and I gasped as I hit the floor. He took a minute to adjust his tie and straighten his jacket, and then he was gone. The entire encounter lasted less than two minutes.

I gasped for breath, scared out of my mind, and began to sob. I knew I had to get myself under control in the few minutes before Mase got home, but it was too late for that. I looked up and he was walking through the doorway.

"Lanie, honey, what's wrong?" He rushed to my side. "What happened?"

And without thinking about how it might sound, I blurted out everything. I was not thinking clearly, and it wasn't the way I planned to tell him, but I couldn't stop once I started. I sobbed and cried through the entire story, including the senator's threats. I showed him the copies of the birth certificates and when I was finished, he didn't ask any questions, he just sat next to me on the floor, quietly, but I could feel the rage building. I could tell he was processing everything I told him— his face tensed, and his eyes clouded. He looked like a different person.

He took my hand softly in his. "Are you okay?" He brushed his hand through my hair.

"I think so. But, Mase, he really scared me."

"I'll take care of it, don't worry," he said. "I promise."

Then, abruptly, he stood and said, "I love you and I'll be back later."

"Where are you going?" I asked, chasing after him, but he didn't answer. He got in his truck and sped out of the driveway.

****

I was a nervous wreck waiting for Mase to come home. I texted him a couple times, but he didn't respond. I tried cleaning up around the house a bit and was randomly texting with Leese, who was doing her best to try and help calm me.

After two hours, ten minutes and thirty-six seconds, he returned.

"I'm sorry," he said. "I needed to think."

"I understand."

"I went to confront my father, but I couldn't find him."

Thank God.

"If he ever lays another hand on you, I will kill him. I'm not ruling it out now."

I think he meant it.

"I think we need to call the police," he added.

"I don't know about that. It would be my word against his and is that the way you want the world to find out that West isn't your son?"

He walked to the fridge and took out a beer.

"Come sit with me on the porch," he said, and I followed him outside.

"When I couldn't find my father, I went to see Bella. It was bad."

He went on to describe that at first, she denied everything. He was so enraged he not only frightened her, he scared himself, and she called the sheriff. Fortunately, it was Robby John who showed up and he was able to calm the situation to some degree. She finally told him that it was Olivia's idea for her to come back to Clarksville, just as we thought, to break up our relationship, but that Olivia had no idea West was the senator's son. Bella went on to say it was the senator's idea to say the boy was Mase's and that he would hold that card until he needed to use it or unless she and Mase got back together. Bella said Olivia was none the wiser. She also said she still loved Mase and could they please try again. Then Mase said thoughtfully, "no one even considers West in any of their decisions. It's like he isn't even a person."

The entire story made me physically sick and emotionally sad, and I started to cry. It was the very last thing I wanted to do, but I couldn't help myself. The tears came so quickly I couldn't stop them. Mase pulled me close, so my face was buried in his chest and stroked my hair.

"I'm so sorry," I cried.

My nose was running, and I wiped it on his shirt. I looked up at his face. The face I loved. The face that was in pain.

"You look like a raccoon," he whispered. He pulled me tightly into him and kissed me tenderly. "And I love you."

Chapter 21

Nothing good ever comes from a knock on the door in the middle of the night.

It had been an emotionally trying few days, as we had to tell West (and Zoey) what we found out, because Bella refused. She finally agreed to be present after much pressure and after Mase had to question her love for her son, with Mase and me, when my thoughtful and gracious husband had to tell this little boy the truth. Mase still hadn't been able to contact his father and was told by everyone he spoke to that, "The senator is away for an indefinite time working on a pressing business matter." We had no idea whether Bella had spoken to him about what was happening today, or if Olivia had been clued in, as she was out of town as well, and not returning Mase's calls.

We met at Bella's because she insisted, only after she had the nerve to lecture Mase on what behavior she would not tolerate, and to which Mase cutoff immediately. It was the first time I had been to her house. My heart tightened as we climbed the few porch stairs and knocked on her front door because this is where I assumed she and Mase had their thing, and it irritated and saddened me to be there. But this wasn't about me and because he thought it would be good for West to be in a comfortable and familiar place for this discussion (and basically it was all Bella would agree to do), I wanted to be as supportive as I could, realizing that any chance Bella may have had with Mase had completely evaporated due to her own deceit.

Her house was on the smaller side but exquisitely decorated with antique furniture and rugs. It was painted in neutral tones with accent pillows and rugs adding strategically placed splashes of color. There was no evidence a young boy lived there. The Senator took very good care of her; that was obvious.

Without speaking to either of us, Bella let us in and retrieved West from his room. He bounced in and sat between Mase and me on the couch. Bella sat across from us on an antique Paris Accent chair.

"Hey, Dad," West said, his chipper disposition on display. "Hey Lanie," he added and then after a look from his mother, added, "I mean Miss Lanie."

I had no idea what Mase planned to say, but I was certain that he had given it serious thought.

"Hi, son," Mase began.

I almost lost it then.

"I came to talk to you," he said, "because your mom and I found out some important information that involves you."

"What important information?" he asked.

"Well…" Mase paused and took a deep breath. I could tell he was trying to keep it together.

"I want you to know that I love you very much, and that's not going to change," he said, choking up. "But we recently found out that I'm not really your biological father like your mom and I thought."

I loved him more in that moment than I can express.

"What do you mean?"

The look of concern on his face was heartbreaking.

Bella interjected. "What he means, honey, is that I thought he was your father, but he's not."

West started to panic.

"But I love you. I don't want another dad," he cried, and he hugged Mase tightly.

I quietly wiped the tears that I tried silently to control.

Bella was stoic.

"It's okay," Mase reassured him. "I'm not your biological father, but I will always be your dad. And I am not going anywhere, son. Nothing between us is going to change."

West was old enough to understand much of this conversation, and he had a few questions.

"I don't understand," he cried, "Who is my father?"

We could hear a pin drop. The look on Bella's face was undisguised panic.

"I'm not sure," she choked out. "I'm so sorry, honey," she said, and she seemed genuine and remorseful in her tone with him. In that moment she became human as she embraced West and kissed the top of his head tenderly.

"No one is perfect, and your mom made a mistake thinking it was me," Mase reinforced.

"Well this is a big one and I don't want another dad," West huffed, stomped back into his room and slammed the door.

Mase turned to face Bella and in the sternest tone I had ever heard him use, said, "You better figure out how to tell him who his father is because he's going to keep asking. You better think about it hard."

He knocked on West's door and spent several more minutes with him alone and that left Bella and me in awkward silence. I had no use for her whatsoever. Not only because she slept with my husband which obviously would be enough for any woman to despise her, but she created a relationship between Mase and a vulnerable child, her child, for her own gain. As far as I was concerned, the satisfaction I got from seeing her true colors paled in comparison to watching Mase and West struggle with her lie. I scrolled on my phone to avoid having to look at her.

After a couple of minutes, she started to say something.

"Don't," I said and cut her off completely.

Mase emerged from the bedroom and without saying a word, took my hand and we left.

****

Telling Zoey was easier, but she had her own drama happening.

"Geez, Mom, what the hell?"

"Z."

"Sorry, but what the hell?"

"I know, it's crazy, but it's true."

"And RJ works for that scumball."

That was the extent of Zoey's response to the revelation of West's parenthood. It had been about a week since I gave Mase the news, and the senator was due back in town within the next couple of days, according to his people. Zoey was interested in Mase's thoughts and reaction to this bombshell because she hadn't been around much with school in full swing. I described what I saw, throwing in an expletive here and there, giving her the play by play of one of the toughest things I have ever witnessed.

"That bitch," she said. It was a common refrain.

"Oh, I broke up with RJ today," Zoey offered, as if it was the next logical step in our conversation.

I can't say I was surprised. Ever since he changed his college plans without involving her in a decision about their future, she had been struggling to find a way to be okay with his, in her words, "lack of consideration" for her.

"I'm so sorry, honey. How are you feeling? How is he?"

"It's weird, you know. . . it's not really real yet, I guess."

I nodded and put Clark in his highchair because he was reaching for my glass—his signal that he needed something to eat.

"How is RJ?"

"He cried."

I felt bad for him. He knew Z very well so it surprised us all when he made such a huge decision about their future without at least asking for her input.

"He apologized, he asked me to forgive him and, Mom, he kind of begged me not to break up with him. I almost didn't. But if he didn't even ask my opinion about something that completely changes our future, how can I trust him to make good decisions for our family one day?

"That's a reasonable question. Maybe you just need some time to think about things."

"Yeah, that's what he said."

She kissed the back of the baby's head and withdrew toward her room.

Once she was gone, I wept as I thought back on our first encounter with RJ on that steamy summer day when we made our inaugural appearance in Banjoland. She and RJ had been inseparable since then and he was a fixture in our family. He was like a son to me, and this did not feel like a teen break-up. Zoey was not one to make impulsive decisions and she never could reconcile RJ's lack of consideration for her, so while I hoped they could work things out I knew in my heart that this was more than a separation, it was a divorce.

****

After one of the most relaxing family dinners we'd had in a while, I offered to get the dishes while Mase and West discussed his ammo purchases and headed to his room. Mase had struggled when he first found out about West's paternity. He would rage about the situation and then he would cry about it. It was gut wrenching to see him suffering and to struggle to figure out what was best for West and our family. He cut off contact with Bella unless it was absolutely necessary and chose to contact West directly by text or phone he bought for him because of this situation.

"How is he going to handle it when he finds out we are brothers?" Mase lamented.

I did my best to be supportive, but I had no idea what Mase would do when he came face to face with his father, and it wouldn't be long before that happened and before the entire community found out about this colossal farce. That hadn't happened yet and Mase was much calmer when West was with us. He was trying very hard to show West that nothing would be different between them, and I could see West responding to his effort.

I finished cleaning up and took a shower and once Mase finished with West and Clark's bath routine, brought the baby in for a kiss, he returned to our bedroom ready for action. We got cozy and settled in for a Netflix documentary (I love documentaries) and the doorbell rang. I grabbed my robe and followed my husband, one leg in and one leg out of his boxers, curious about who would be at our door at the time when most families were settling in for the night. Mase flipped on the porch light and opened the door to find Robby John standing there, hat in his hand.

"Sorry to disturb y'all," he said, "I know it's after business hours."

"It's okay, Robbie John, how can we help?" Mase asked.

"Do you know where your son is?" he asked.

That was an odd question.

"Which one?" was Mase's response and was the first time publicly I'd heard him acknowledge that he had two sons.

"West."

"Yes, he's upstairs, why?"

West had been very clingy to Mase since everything hit the fan, and because of that had been spending more time with us than usual. He was such a sweet kid, and it hurt my heart for both of them that Mase wasn't his biological father.

"Are you sure?"

"Yes, I'm sure. What is this about?"

I sprinted up the stairs to confirm, even though I was certain he was in his room, just to verify and lay my eyes on him. I knocked on the door and peered in to see West, donned in headphones with a controller in his hands, giving commands to his online troops. He briefly acknowledged me and I gave a quick wave and headed back down the stairs.

By the short time it took me to return, the two long-time friends were standing in silence.

"What's going on?" I asked, the tension between them noticeable.

They were both quiet.

"Mase?"

"Bella's dead," he said flatly. "Someone killed her." Before I could begin to comprehend this, he added, "And we are suspects."

"People of interest," Robbie interjected.

People of interest?

"What does that mean?" I blurted into the awkwardness around me.

Robby explained that Bella was found murdered, and although he couldn't give us any details, they were sure it was murder and we, along with the other people of interest, were being advised not to leave the county without letting law enforcement know beforehand.

"I'm really sorry about all this," he said, but Mase shut the door on him before he finished speaking.

"That was harsh," I said. "He was just doing his job."

"I don't care," Mase said angrily. "I'm tired of dealing with anything related to that woman, dead or alive."

Noticing the look on my face, he added, "And no, I didn't kill her."

Oh my God. I am so relieved—not that he didn't kill her, and that's certainly a good thing—but that she's gone. I can't say that out loud, of course, because there is still a little boy who will be without his mom for the rest of his life and that is truly very sad.

Chapter 22

I had never been a person of interest before, except possibly for a couple of guys I dated over the years, and that was brief interest, so this was new for me. And as you might expect in a small town, news travels like lightning.

"I'm glad she's dead," Leese said as we took our regular jog around the wooded trail.

"I wouldn't say that very loudly, or you'll be a person of interest, too," I joked.

I wasn't the least bit worried about police interest in me because I knew I was innocent, which may have been naïve, but nonetheless I was more interested in who actually killed her and why. While we chatted and jogged, we came across the regulars who decided rather than just jog by and wave, as is the norm, they needed to stop and try to get some gossip fodder.

"Hey, ladies! Hey!"

Oh good God, it was one of Olivia's friends and tattle-tale extraordinaire, Lucy Lovelace, and every single time I heard her name I thought we were referring to a porn star. Even though Lucy could have easily used the exercise equipment at the Club, she ran on the trail because she liked to be seen. I had to give it to her that she was in excellent shape, but she'd had so much plastic surgery that her face didn't look right on her body. She didn't care though. She got plenty of attention from men of all kinds because she was a wealthy widow. Lisa and I tried to act engrossed in our conversation so that she would run on by, but there was no way to avoid her. She literally ran right between us and started asking questions until we finally stopped.

"Hey, Lucy," we said in unison.

"Hey, ladies. I just wanted to check and see how y'all are doing, you know, because of everything that is happening."

The look in her eyes was like that of a child waiting to unwrap a present.

"Everything's good," I answered, while Lisa rolled her eyes with no discretion. But that was not enough.

"So what do they know?" she asked. "Who do you think did it? What does Mason think? I bet he's upset that his child's mother has been murdered."

Mase was not overly upset, and it surprised me a little because at one time he cared very much for his son's mother. I was afraid to say out loud that he was probably relieved she was dead, and I guarded my words carefully.

"We're all adjusting. Thanks for your interest."

With that we took off and without speaking another word, sprinted the last half mile of the dirt path until we were gasping for breath in the parking lot.

****

Mase and I made an appointment with an attorney that Whit recommended, because he wanted to be sure we hired someone completely free of connections to the family. At this point Mase said he didn't know who to trust and I couldn't blame him. Ad did a little research on the guy Whit suggested and gave us the nod to go forward.

"He is a high-powered guy, and some of my friends in Congress have used him for a variety of cases. He usually doesn't do defense work because he prefers cases where the high dollars are, but when he does, he wins," Ad told us before we hired him. Our meeting was scheduled for tomorrow morning and we were still in the dark about what happened to Bella and who else was a person of interest. The number one priority for us at the moment was West and helping him adjust. It was also in the back of my mind, and I'm sure in Mase's, that with Bella dead, Senator Downes was West's next of kin, and as his biological father, would have all the rights and entitlements to what happened with West. To our knowledge, the only ones that knew the truth about his paternity were our small group, Whit and the senator. Mase and his father had not had the reckoning that was coming because the senator made himself unavailable. This let us know he had a calculated plan to respond in his time now that he knew Mase knew his secret. West didn't talk about it outside our house, and he didn't know who his biological father was anyway. As far as he was concerned, nothing had changed in his relationship with Mase. And now with Bella dead, we felt that keeping things as stable as possible was the best thing we could do for him.

Lisa and Ad came by to grill and have a few drinks because they were who they are to us. It was nice that we could relax and speak freely, after having to guard everything I said to everyone every day just to make sure I didn't say anything that could be misinterpreted. It was quite a challenge for me since I have difficulty filtering what I say anyway, and in all truthfulness, an area in which I needed to improve.

We sat on the swing drinking champagne while our men grilled and talked college football. Fall was here, another football season, hunting had already begun, Z's birthday and the opening of dove season bash were all upon us once again. It seemed to come around more quickly this year and with things up in the air, it was hard to think about creating the same fun we'd had at these events for so many years.

"So, any new ideas?" Leese asked, swallowing the last of her champagne. We had been debating this ad nauseum since we first found out Bella was dead.

"Not really," I said. "Still think it's probably the senator, you know, because he is violent and has buried at least one body. I mean, he did have a motive."

"You're probably right," she said, but added, "Maybe it was Olivia. Who knows?"

"I don't know. We'll see what the attorney says tomorrow. Hopefully he can fill in the gaps for us."

The screen door swung open, and Zoey appeared holding Clark, who was chattering away in his own language, occasionally spouting a familiar word. His birthday was coming, too, after the first of the year. His baby hair had fallen out revealing reddish brown, curly locks that made him look older than he was. His arms and legs looked like sausages, but the pediatrician assured me he was well within his desired weight range, and that he would grow into his body. He was toddling, and he could clap his hands and wave bye-bye. It seems hilarious when I think about how proud I was of this— like no other baby would ever reach these milestones— but it was the first time I created a person with someone I loved. I looked for myself in him, just like I did Z, but I also looked and saw Mase in him, too, and I am always happy when that happens.

"Your son is hungry." She handed him over to me.

"Why don't you feed him?" I asked, because she enjoyed feeding him, and she could make him laugh like no one else.

"Can't– have a date for the fall formal." She disappeared without discussion back into the house.

"A date?" Leese said.

"News to me."

A few minutes later, Greggins pulled into the driveway in an old Chevy Dooley.

"Where's your gal?" I asked.

"Broke up," he said.

"Happens," Leese added. "Your truck?"

"Sure is," he answered proudly.

He wouldn't be old enough to drive for another year and a half. No one commented on that fact, as it was typical for teens in Banjoland to drive underage, as long as they stayed in the local area.

"You look nice, Greg. What's the occasion?"

"Hot date."

Just then Z materialized and walked through the open screen door. She was coiffed, dressed and perfumed to the max. She had gone above and beyond her normal date look.

"Holy smokes," Mase said. "Who's the lucky guy?"

"I am," Greggins said, and took Zoey's hand as she walked down the steps, across the drive and up into his truck.

We were dumbstruck until Ad said, "This can't be good."

They were gone five minutes when Z FaceTimed me from the WaWa gas station down the dirt road.

"You should have seen the look on your faces." She laughed, with Greg giving a thumbs-up in the background while pumping gas. She was so amused with herself she snorted a little. "We're not on a date," she laughed, "remember my car is in the shop."

I had completely forgotten.

"Not that she could do better," Greg chimed in as he climbed into the driver's seat.

She ended her call, still laughing at us and I was more relieved than I could explain.

****

We drove to Tallahassee the next morning because that's where the lawyer was, and I was glad it was a distance from Banjoland for a couple of reasons. First, I thought it would help us keep things as private as we could—no nosy neighbors that spy us going into a law office and then spreading truth and fiction regarding said visit—and also because I felt like we were out of the senator's reach. I wasn't naïve enough to think he didn't have contacts in the Capital City. As a matter of fact, he had many significant political connections there, but he also had vociferous opposition. With campaigning for the new term gaining steam, alliances were forming. Ad assured us we could trust this man.

Tallahassee is an old Florida city, full of huge oak trees dripping with Spanish moss—more of a Georgia feel than a Florida feel I have been told—with a significant Spanish architectural presence. I didn't expect to spend time here now that RJ decided not to go to FSU, but it was a pleasant change of scenery and a welcome time alone with my man.

"You okay, babe?"

"Yeah." He reached for my hand. "I'll be glad when

this is all over. And Lane," he paused for a moment, "I have a meeting with my father when we get back tonight."

"A meeting with your father?" I repeated. Mase had been trying to get in contact with him for over a month—since this whole façade with West was exposed. But as we have always known, no one (even family) gets to the senator without his knowledge and approval.

"Yes. Interestingly, he had his people contact me to set it up."

I was silent as I mulled over this new information.

"And Lane, please don't mention this to the attorney. I'm not sure how much I am going to disclose and at what time."

I nodded in agreement but wondered to myself why we wouldn't be completely transparent with our attorney.

We pulled into the underground parking garage of a modernesque building near Duval Street that was in the middle of a chain of parks designed to provide residents with live oaks, azaleas, and lush green space.

Our attorney's name was Allen Gordon Walker, and his office was on the 3rd floor. We used the stairs instead of the elevator, and when we entered his lobby, we were greeted by a young, perky intern who introduced herself as Annalise. She offered us foreign coffee, a variety of cold drink options, and a gourmet snack platter. We politely declined and before we could get comfortable in our lush surrounds, and discuss said surroundings, Allen Gordon Walker's secretary, Mary Neal, ushered us back to his office where we waited outside the door for his signal to enter.

Mase strode confidently toward AGW, holding my

hand until we stood directly in front of this odd-looking character. He was short and fat and not just a little; he was rotund. He was completely bald with thick, black-rimmed glasses that magnified his eyes, and I chuckled to myself because he reminded me of Mr. Magoo.

He rose from behind his massive desk and held out his hand.

"Allen Gordon Walker. Nice to meet you both."

"Mason Downes," and nodding toward me, "my wife Melanie," said Mase, and we all shook hands.

"Have a seat." AGW pointed to formal, high back chairs a few feet from his desk. "And let's start from the beginning."

Chapter 23

I wanted to go with Mase to meet his father, but he wouldn't let me. He wouldn't even consider it, but he did promise he would maintain his composure and that it was time they met and "put our cards on the table." I thought that if I was with him it might help keep things calmer, although there was no reason whatsoever why it would.

I finally agreed to stay home if he would take Adam along, but as Mase pointed out and I should have remembered, given Ad's history with the senator, that didn't seem like a good idea either. Mase promised to remain calm, and he had noticeably, outwardly, calmed down since he first learned that he wasn't West's biological father. He had decided, with my full support, to be as much of a father to West as he could be, especially now that the boy's mother was dead.

The meeting with his father was at 7:00pm, and Lisa agreed to keep me company while we waited for whatever was to come of this encounter. Because Leese and Ad both understood the gravity of what could happen, Ad decided he would follow unbeknownst to Mase, at a distance, and stay close by in case things got out of hand. Before I might have thought this was a bit dramatic, but after all I had experienced in Banjoland, I realized that the drama could be real and having Ad close brought me a little peace.

"So what did your attorney say?" Leese asked, while

she swung on the swing holding a cooing Clark.

"Not much," I said. "We had to formally retain him so that he could request all the information the police and detectives had pertaining to Bella's death."

"Is West coping any better?" she asked.

It had been a tough adjustment.

"Still some good days and bad days," I offered. "We're supposed to meet with the attorney again next week when he has all the information. Until then, he told us to 'live quietly'."

"Interesting," she said and then switched gears completely. "So what's with Zoey and RJ? Anything new?"

"She hasn't said anything lately and I don't want to ask too many questions, you know? I'm not sure she knows what she's doing as far as he goes."

We laughed at Z's humorous prank about her going on a date with Greggins and what a disaster that could have been and Lisa added "they actually look oddly good together, except he's so much younger than her."

I nodded in agreement while I thought about that and until my mind wandered back to Mase. I wondered why the senator instigated this meeting, but I knew inherently, as with everything he did, it was for his gain. Ad texted periodically to let us know he was eating a po-boy sandwich across from the senator's office, or with some random comment about people he observed on the street. I appreciated his effort, but every time he texted, I braced for some unpleasant revelation. Finally, after an hour and a half, we got the all clear from Ad that the meeting had ended, and he was on his way back.

Not long after the call, our porch chat was interrupted by the sound of Ad skidding into the driveway. He flew up the stairs and onto the porch, tossed his keys at the table, grabbed Clark and acted like he'd been with us all night. Clark was oblivious, repeated his name and grabbed for his phone.

Mase arrived shortly after, grabbed an icy cold beer out of the cooler on the porch, loosened his tie and took a seat so that together we all formed a square and where we eagerly awaited the details of his meeting.

We waited silently as he took a long swallow.

"Well," he began, "it was interesting, I'll say that much."

It *was* interesting. As Mase gave us the play-by-play account of their conversation, I visualized them—the senator sitting in his oversized office chair, legs crossed, smoking a high-end cigar and showing no emotion—simply stating facts. Mase pacing, peppering him with questions and trying to keep his emotions in check. "I wasn't surprised he was so candid and emotionless," said Mase, "I've seen him like that my entire life, but the way he was recounting what happened like it was simply a story he was telling that had no impact on anyone seemed arrogant even for him." Mase took another swallow of his beer, wiped his lips with his sleeve and paused, like he was replaying the conversation with his father in his head. He went on to describe that after he confronted his father, not only about West but about his visit to me, the senator admitted when he found out Olivia had arranged for Bella to come back to town, he thought it would be in everyone's best interest for Mase to be the boy's father, given that Olivia was unaware of his true paternity—and further, he had no problem at all with Olivia's meddling—in fact, he agreed with her ultimate goal of reuniting Mase and Bella since it served his purpose of disguising the fact that he is West's father.

He stood, nonchalantly added "and then I punched him in the mouth" as tossed his bottle in the can next to table and popped open another before returning to his chair, and that was then I noticed the swollen knuckles on his right hand. "I told him if he ever touched you again," looking directly at me, "they wouldn't find his body."

Leese and I made eye contact. We were speechless.

"There's more," he said before anyone could put a sentence together. "He made a proposition once he gathered himself."

When he finished explaining what the senator proposed, my first thought was it that it just seemed too easy.

Basically, the senator proposed a deal. Mase could continue to act as West's father and Senator Downes would sign over his paternal rights, all on the down low, in exchange for Mase's silence about the boy's true paternity, to everyone, including silence with regards to Olivia.

His final pitch for the deal, according to Mase was that "no one would know" and "what West needs now is stability."

"Except," Lisa interjected softly, "West already knows you aren't his father."

"But," Ad continued as soon as she finished, "West doesn't know who his father is, and if Mase formally, legally becomes his father, then for all intents and purposes, he *is* West's father."

"Uhm, Whit knows, remember?" I added almost as an afterthought.

We mulled this around for a while, throwing out

pros and cons.

"What if he tells Olivia," Ad said. "Everyone knows they are lovers."

Leese and I busted out laughing at his use of "lovers" to describe their relationship.

"Ewe," Lisa said.

Mase shook his head and chuckled. It was nice to see him smile.

After discussing this for a while we decided that we couldn't control whether Whit ever said anything, and if he decided to hold this over the senator's head that was between them because Mase would still be West's legal father. Interestingly, the senator never asked how we found out the truth.

****

"I'm not getting sucked up in the drama," Z reported, when I asked her what was going on with RJ. We hadn't had an "update" on her life since they broke up, save a few snippets here and there because she seemed to be living in a constant state of motion.

The volume of her curls made her face look tiny in the morning. It was football season and as an upper classman, she had school responsibilities that sometimes called for an early Saturday wake-up. She plopped onto a stool next to the kitchen bar and began licking the cream out of her favorite Cannoli that Leese had dropped off the day before and waited for me to pour our coffee.

"Explain," I said, topping it off with some whipped cream.

"I mean, you know he's been dating that Senior—the one that was in the homecoming court last year, right?"

"Well, I heard something from someone at the

grocery store the other day. . ." she interrupted "He doesn't even like her. He used to say she was a snob and that she was stuck on herself."

"But as I recall, she had a huge crush on him, right?"

"Yeah, whatever. He's playing a game and I'm not playing."

"I'm sorry, Z, I know this must be tough."

"Whatever. I'm over it."

And with that, she went to get Clark who was waking and making his presence known.

****

It didn't take much at all to have West's paternity officially changed to Mase—an out-of-town meeting at a lawyer's office, some notarized paperwork to file with court, (again out of town), a new birth certificate and that was it. West was ecstatic. I was happy about it, too. Since he had been with us full-time it felt like he completed our family. He was bright and funny, and genuinely a sweet boy, and we got to see glimpses of that as he continued to deal with his mom's death. I was glad we could be there for him, and he could be there for us, in this difficult time. What I also found interesting was that the police were unaware of this "transaction" or that there was any question at all regarding West's paternity.

"Why is this a secret?" I asked Mase.

"The less anyone knows the more likely it will never come up," he said flatly.

"But, I mean, with the investigation and everything, wouldn't this matter?"

"The less anyone knows the more likely it will never come up," he said once more.

This seemed ridiculous to me. Legal paperwork was filed. I mean, J. Michael found out West's paternity for us—why wouldn't the police be able to do the same thing?

"Because they would have no reason to look," Mase said.

It was apparent to me that I didn't have all the information that Mase had, and that he wasn't interested in discussing it further, so I let the subject drop for the moment.

****

I felt like a frequent flyer at the police station, given the several times I had been there. It was weirdly comforting in that it was familiar.

Allen Gordon Walker advised that we meet there rather than have the investigators come to our home, and that way we could have control and leave whenever we chose. He also advised that depending on this "conference", we might need separate attorneys, given that we were both people of interest and that it would be a conflict for him to represent us both. I didn't think too much about that until I experienced this meeting, which felt much more like an interrogation. AGW advised us not to say anything unless he gave us the okay, but to listen to what the investigators had to say, as this meeting was to get everyone to show their hands.

When it was over, they directed us to leave. I was completely drained and overwhelmed with emotion. Mase held my hand and led me outside and across the street to our bench under the towering oak, while we waited for Allen Gordon Walker to help us make sense of everything. We sat quietly until Mase finally uttered a word.

He choked out a muffled, "I'm so sorry, Lane. . ." but I couldn't respond.

Allen appeared a few minutes later and after reviewing with us some of the key information that we heard, and how he thought we could respond, he said, "Lanie, obviously you will need separate representation. I have one of my partners on standby and I'd be glad to set up a meeting as soon as possible." His voice faded away as I thought about my children.

I didn't speak for the entire ride home, and once we got there, I immediately left to find Lisa, who was babysitting Clark and waiting for AJ and West to return from basketball practice.

"Mommy's here," she sang while my handsome chunk reached out for me. Every time I saw him it made my heart swell. As corny as that sounds.

Lisa handed me a bottle and poured us each some champagne while we sat on our perch overlooking her manicured yard and I detailed our meeting with the investigators.

"Holy shit," she said, surprised and bewildered. "I hope you have your own attorney."

"I do." I sighed while my baby guzzled like he had never eaten before. "I mean I haven't hired him yet, but I guess I'll use Allen Gordon's partner."

I was still in shock. I am not sure what I was expecting, but I was certainly not expecting to find out that Bella was pregnant when she was killed. The autopsy indicated that she was in her second trimester, approximately twenty weeks along. This meant that she got pregnant around the time that she and Mase had their one night together—if one night was truly all they had.

The thought made me sick. I was doing my best to put that episode behind me/us and I believed that Mase was sincere in his desire to be with me—not that Bella was an option anymore—but I felt this strongly before she died anyway. All this did was bring up everything I was trying to forget, and no matter how hard I tried, all I could do was imagine what life would have been like if she had lived and actually was the mother of one of Mase's children. At no time did I know that she was pregnant, but detectives didn't know I didn't know, so this made me (and Mase) suspects because they said this was a motive to kill her. Suddenly my lackadaisical attitude became serious and concerned. I knew I didn't kill her, but someone did, and her pregnancy certainly could have wrecked our lives, at least for a while and so I guess that could be construed as a motive.

There were so many pieces of this puzzle left to figure out. I certainly didn't think Mase was a murderer, but someone killed her. But who, and why? Was it because she was pregnant, or was that even known to the killer?

"There must be more," Leese and I said in unison. There had to be. The senator's involvement had to be more than an altruistic, though self-serving motive to sign over West to Mase—especially with everything that was happening.

"What about Olivia?" Leese threw in. "Why wouldn't she be a person of interest? She could have found out he had an affair with Bella and is West's father."

"That doesn't seem very likely, I mean, she knows he's had affairs during their entire marriage, why would this be the time to kill someone?"

None of this made sense and it made me wonder what else the police knew and were not sharing.

"I'm not sure," Mase said, rubbing his head. The

lines on his forehead crinkled as he pondered out loud. "Our attorneys will be getting all of the evidence that the police have and maybe there will be some clues."

"Well, no one's been arrested yet, so they can't have much, right?"

"Who knows?" Mase replied, throwing up his arms. "They may be following leads and making sure they dot their I's and cross their T's. I know one thing. I'm not going to wait around in limbo to see what happens."

With that statement, he left, and I didn't try to stop him. I wanted some time alone to figure out what was happening and to try and make sense of this circus that had become my life.

Chapter 24

The investigation dragged on. My attorney and AGW's partner, Victor Neumann, said the police had several theories but not much evidence; that they were trying to uncover the smoking gun. Mase said that AGW told him the same thing.

It was difficult to move forward with daily life having this hanging over our heads, and our family was the talk of the town. Even Zoey was getting quizzed at school. Everyone was speculating and offering their opinions and it wasn't long before the national media picked up on the story, primarily because it involved the senator and based on his history, would generate massive TV ratings.

Reporters from all the major networks began to descend on Banjoland once again, billing the story as a continuation of family drama that began years ago. They were showing up at redneck central to get a random person's interview; they were at the high school football game; and they were even staking out the Country Club—where no matter what happened, the Downes family continued to be treated like royalty.

Navigating and protecting West through this ordeal was our biggest challenge, not only because he was a bright child and would catch on quickly to the details of the circumstances surrounding his mother's death, but also because we couldn't shield him from questions at school, and because we couldn't explain why anyone would want to hurt his mom.

"I don't understand, Lanie," he said early on. "Was my mom a bad person?"

His hazel eyes clouded with tears as he waited apprehensively for an answer.

"No, honey," I said, filled with compassion for this boy who was, as we all were, trying to make sense of what happened and the ensuing media fiasco. I pulled him close and softly kissed the top of his head. "She wasn't a bad person. Whoever did this was the bad person."

****

After much debate, we decided to have the annual opening of dove season/Zoey's birthday bash event as we normally would despite everything that was happening for two reasons: Mase thought we needed a good time, and number two, he thought it would be a good distraction. Because it was an annual event that we had choreographed for so long, it didn't take much prep time to get everything in order and unlike the prior year, there would be no descending senators for whom we would need to insure a good time. It would be for us, the locals, and our friends and I found myself looking forward to the diversion.

****

The day was gorgeous, as they usually were in early October, and I think the fact that the air was dryer than the sweltering summer months gave everyone more energy. Lisa came over early to offer help, but what was in actuality an excuse to begin drinking a bit earlier than usual. Zoey and her friends, including RJ (sans gal pal— a wise choice), began setting up the games because the competitive mentality in Banjoland permeated every activity, especially horseshoes. It reminded me of when Zoey was a little girl and I congratulated her for a second-place finish in a 50-yard dash.

"Mom, second place is just the first loser," she said, and she applied this perspective to everything she did in life.

She and her friends took out the four-wheelers and the Mule and began picking up extraneous debris, tree limbs, branches, etc. that had fallen in the windstorm a day earlier. I watched as she acted friendly with RJ and I wondered what she was thinking about him, his new girl, and their future.

"Everything seems so normal," Lisa interrupted.

"It really does," I acknowledged, except for them, and I nodded in the direction of Z and RJ.

"They'll work it out," she said, "like they always do.

I wasn't so sure but chose not to dwell on it and instead tried to focus on what was happening in the moment.

Ad and Mase cruised up on Ad's refurbished (read jacked up redneck style) golf cart, complete with antlers on the front—at Christmastime he would hang ornaments on these—with news.

"So," Mase said, "my contacts downtown tell me that there is a possible break in the case."

Leese and I eagerly waited for him to continue.

"I don't know what it is and neither does he, but I can only think we are very close to having this nightmare over."

I was hopeful for the first time since Bella appeared on the scene that our lives could be calm and peaceful.

The hope was brief. RJ and Z came bolting out of

the woods on a four-wheeler with Greggins on the back and as they got closer we could see he was bleeding profusely from the inside of his upper thigh.

"We can't get the bleeding to stop," Z said urgently.

He had a nasty gash about six inches long and deep enough that we could plainly see it needed stitches.

Ad got the first aid kit from his golf cart, while Greg explained what happened.

"I was clearing out some of the kudzu from the back trail, you know, the one that leads out into the pasture, with a machete," he explained, grimacing while he followed Ad's instructions to keep pressure on it. "The handle snapped off and the blade flung into my leg."

He was visibly in pain, and the blood was soaking through the gauze.

Mase and Ad, followed by Z and RJ, carried him to RJ's truck and set off for the emergency room.

"Never a boring moment," Lisa said.

"I miss those," I joked as I wondered what the breakthrough in the investigation could be and what would happen next.

They kept Greg in the hospital because his blood was not coagulating, and they found he was anemic. They said they wanted to do some more tests, but he shouldn't have to stay very long.

****

Our attorneys scheduled a joint meeting for Mase and me later in the week, and it was there, we presumed, that we would find out the latest information that would hopefully put an end to this drama. I was more than curious to find out who killed Bella and why, and eager to put this entire episode behind us. Interestingly, we found out that there was a press conference regarding the case set for later that same afternoon.

It was difficult to concentrate as the week moved along because the anticipation of receiving information was palpable within the community. The news people were even more visible, which I didn't think was possible, and it was all we could do to avoid showing up to our meeting two hours early.

"Please have a seat," Allen Gordon Walker said as he ushered us into his plush office. Victor Newman, with his Abe Lincoln like beard and black stovetop hat, was already seated and rose when we entered.

"Afternoon." He nodded toward us.

"Before we begin," AGW said, "I need both of y'alls permission to discuss this case in front of each other, as you both have separate representation."

"We agree," we said.

"I'm going to explain where we are in this process, and I want either of you to feel free to stop me at any point if you have any questions. You need to thoughtfully consider the information I am about to give you, as the consequences will be far reaching."

My stomach was in knots.

It didn't take very long at all to understand what he meant by that statement. Olivia had been ruled out as a suspect because the police did not think she had a motive. West's paternity still appeared to be under wraps as far as she was concerned, so it didn't seem like she had any reason to commit a murder. Even if she knew about the senator's affair with Bella, why would she choose this woman to kill? Adding to that there was no physical evidence linking her to the crime.

But this is where things went south, fast.

When questioned by police, Senator Downes

explained that Mase blackmailed him into signing custody of West over to him by threatening to tell Olivia the boy's true paternity and showing her evidence of the thousands of dollars that the senator was giving to Bella on a regular basis. The senator explained that not only would this have been devastating to his marriage, but it would have ruined his chances in the upcoming election. He thought it in his best interests, as well as Olivia and West's, to comply with Mase's demand.

I was dumbfounded. Mase did not comment and remained stone faced as AWG continued.

"There's more. Police have established a motive for the murder was to keep Bella's pregnancy hidden, and there would only be one individual who would primarily benefit from that, and it would be Mason, for the obvious reason."

Mase interjected, "All of this seems speculative to me. What my father said is basically his word against mine, and there is no physical evidence linking me to this crime. It sounds like guesswork, amateur guesswork, to me."

I wondered if Mase did try and blackmail the senator.

"If that's all there is, we'll be leaving," Mase said as he took my hand and stood.

"There's more." Allen Gordan Walker pointed toward our chairs. "It seems that there is security footage that shows you entering Bella's house early on the morning of the day that she was killed."

My chest tightened.

"Yes," Mase confirmed. "I never denied that and I believe I told the police that my son forgot his homework and I stopped by to pick it up for him."

I took a few deep breaths to try and control my growing anxiety.

"But you didn't knock. You let yourself in with a key," the counselor added.

"Yes," he acknowledged. "I wanted to avoid a confrontation with her, as you know by the texts we sent just prior to that. We argued and it was ugly."

He hadn't told me any of this. My rapidly increasing heart rate and rising temperature created beads of sweat on the back of my neck.

It disgusted me that he still had a key to her house. And that I had no idea that he was communicating with her so much.

"Well, as you can see," Victor Neumann chimed in, "now the police have motive and opportunity. . .and there's more."

What more could there be?

He went on to explain that Bella was strangled— which had not been released to us or the public— and that DNA was found on her body that matched Mase's DNA. We had all given samples early on, as encouraged by our attorneys, "if," they said, "you are confident in your innocence."

Mase had no explanation for this and was adamant that he didn't kill her.

"Melanie, you were considered as a possible accessory, but at this point, it doesn't look like they have any way to make that stick."

As if disregarding Mase's denial, Allen Gordon Walker said that they would provide a rigorous defense and that the case had several holes, but his DNA was going to need a plausible reason for appearing on Bella's clothes.

"One more thing," he added. "The police are going to issue a statement proudly announcing an arrest in the case. They would like you to turn yourself in immediately following our meeting, or they will come to your home and make a public spectacle of arresting you. We have been working diligently behind the scenes to get you released on your own recognizance because of your ties to the community and your history of working in law enforcement. You may have to spend a few nights in jail for the publicity it will generate, but that's the best we could do."

I was in shock, and one of the first things that came to my mind was West, and how we would ever explain this to him. Z would be on Mase's side no matter what happened—his guilt or innocence would not matter.

Mase turned himself in and the media were relentless. They shouted all kinds of comments at us as we entered the police station, including:

"What does it feel like to be married to a murderer?"

I did my best to ignore them, but that one shook me right down to my core. I didn't know what to do or what to think or even what was real.

Chapter 25

"Greggins has MDS, Mom."

"MDS?"

"Myelodysplastic Syndrome. Leukemia. They found abnormal blood counts in his blood work. It explains why he is tired all the time and why he bruises so easily," she said. "They are referring him to an oncologist to see what kind of treatment he needs."

"Wow. How is he? How's Aideen?"

"He's the same as usual and she's pretty stressed. RJ and I are going to bring them supper and see what the plan for his treatment will be."

I let the reference to RJ go unmentioned, and shot Aideen a text that said I was thinking of them, and that I would stop by later with RJ and Z.

"Thanks so much," she texted back. "I'm freaking out."

****

Olivia and the senator were putting on a public display of unity and dismay that their son would be accused of such a crime, and I think they were enjoying every bit of the attention. The senator gave an exclusive interview to Fox News—ironically the outlet he railed against when he was on trial—appearing as a caring and loving patriarch who couldn't understand how such a terrible tragedy had occurred, referring both to Bella's murder and Mason's arrest.

"I just don't understand how this could happen," he said. "This isn't the son that I know."

Olivia and her minions went about business as usual, lunching at the Club and playing tennis daily.

Mase was able to negotiate a release from jail after a few days, and we both sat down with West to try and help him understand something that neither one of us understood.

"But Dad, if you didn't do it, why did the police arrest you? They're the good guys, right?"

Mase was patient and kind in his response. "Well, son," he began, "sometimes even the good guys make mistakes."

****

We rode over to Aideen's that evening without Mase because he and Ad were working on something related to the case and that was the priority. It was a cooler evening than usual, and RJ had the windows down.

"Ray (Zoey affectionately called RJ Ray sometimes), roll the windows up, it's cold outside."

"It's not cold," he said, "you're just too thin."

They bantered like always, and I really had no idea what was going on between them.

Aideen and Greg were inside mulling over online research about MDS and discussing what they found with each other.

"Hey, all." Aideen got up to properly greet us.

"Sit." I helped Z unpack the delicacies from KFC, a special request from Greg.

We gathered around the table to share a meal, fellowship and to support our friends. This was something we didn't do much in SoHo, as we were much younger then with different priorities. One of the things I learned living in Banjoland was the importance of community. Even in this trying time with the murder, our friends banded around us and supported us and cared for us when we weren't sure how to do it for ourselves.

The treatment recommendation for Greggins was a stem cell transplant because he was young and in good health. What they needed to do was find a donor so that he wouldn't have to be placed on a list that could potentially take years to match him with a suitable candidate. The plan was to engage the community so that people would volunteer to be tested and that way a donor could be found much more quickly, hopefully, than to wait in line on the national register. His prognosis with the transplant was guarded but good.

Z, Greg and RJ made plans to create an awareness program and each agreed to get tested themselves to set an example. I was proud of them. They were motivated and as they did in so many other areas of life, they not only took control, they took action. Immediate family is usually where the process begins, and Aideen had already been tested. As expected, she was a partial match, but not the best match for him, so the search continued. The rest of us would be tested ASAP, and we would educate the community on the process as well.

****

Mase and Allen Gordon Walker were busy preparing his defense, as the prosecutors were preparing to take his case to the grand jury. AGW felt like they had as solid a defense as they could, given the DNA situation, but Mase was not leaving things as they were. He was not a passive man by nature, and he sure wasn't going to let his future rest in someone else's hands, no matter how experienced those hands were. He and Ad hired J. Michael Phillips; the same investigator Whit recommended I use to get the details about West's paternity. Since Ad knew of him and had done some background research of his own, he felt like J. would be able to help. That's all Mase would tell me because, he said, he wanted me to be able to honestly say that I didn't know what he was doing if I was ever asked. That made sense to me, but at the same time, the nagging thought of his DNA on Bella's clothes made me sick when I thought about it.

"What did he say when you asked him?" Lisa pondered out loud.

"He said he didn't know how it got there, but that I could 100% trust he was telling me the truth even though he knew that was asking a lot," I responded.

We both knew that was a lame answer even if it was the truth, and it made me uneasy. His delivery was believable, but the fact remained that his DNA was on Bella's dress and as far as I knew, there was only one way for it to get there. I was torn between feeling like an idiot for seeming to ignore the obvious and feeling deep down that he was telling me the truth, but I decided to follow Lisa's advice and wait to see how things played out before making any permanent decisions.

Ad and Mase were in the garage, working on Ad's truck and discussing plans for Mase's defense strategy if after the grand jury met tomorrow, he was indicted. AGW said an indictment was likely because the prosecution doesn't have to prove its case, and it's a rather perfunctory step toward a trial.

****

Zoey and RJ had been spending time together,

especially since Greg had been diagnosed with MDS. I hadn't seen his girlfriend around and I avoided asking any questions, even though I was curious and wondered If he and Z could "just be friends" given their history and his involvement with the senator, whose campaign was gearing up and while he was using all the publicity from Mase's arrest as a chance to spew his message to the masses. I was still surprised that a convicted felon could run for congress, but apparently it was more common than one would think, and now that he had access to the bank's money as Chairman, he was considered an asset to his party. RJ was heavily involved in his campaign, as he was promised, and he seemed to relish the experience. He maintained his position at the bank, and Z was on course for her future at Florida State. Given that our experience was being scrutinized not only by our town, but by the national media, I thought we were managing fairly well.

****

Clark and I were waiting on Leese to take our daily cruise around the walking/biking trail that meandered through the sports complex near the edge of town. The trail was packed dirt flanked by pines and elms and it's shade provided a slight respite from the heat of the day. We tried to change up the times a bit to avoid the "accidental" run-ins from the local do-gooders or from random media people. I was pushing Clark on a baby swing near the tennis courts when my phone dinged with a text.

Great. Leese can't make it and I'm on my own.

It was from Z: "Mom, come home ASAP. Not an emergency, but important."

I immediately called her but she didn't respond, so I

texted Leese and had her meet me at the house instead of at the trail. She arrived ahead of me, and as I cruised into the driveway it was all I could do to keep from thinking the worst. I unbuckled Clark from his car seat and I guess the look on my face scared him because he let out a whale of a scream and I stopped dead in my tracks. I took a moment to breathe—somewhat comforted that Z said whatever this was wasn't an emergency— slid a bottle in Clark's mouth, which pacified him immediately, and marched up the steps to whatever important news Z had to share.

"You better sit down for this," Lisa said. She took the baby from my arms and handed me an alcoholic drink.

Zoey didn't waste any time.

"Mom, you know we all have been trying to find a blood donor match for Greggins," she started, "so a bunch of us got tested to show our community that there was nothing to it and to set a good example." She continued, "Well, I got my results back today and not only am I a donor match for him. . ." she paused. . . "here," and she handed me a piece of paper.

No one spoke as I read and then re-read the report.

Zoey explained very slowly, like I was mentally challenged or deaf.

"It looks like I am his sister."

"Well, obviously, it has to be a mistake," I said dismissively, "you just need to get another, accurate test."

Lisa took it from there. "Maybe not," she said gently. "Zoey has two biological parents."

I thought for a minute and remembered what Aideen had said, which wasn't much, about Greggins' father, and that he wasn't a "nice guy."

"Oh my God!" I said as my thoughts crystalized.

Lisa squeezed my hand tightly, signaling me to think about what I said next.

"Mom, could it be possible?"

We had been careful with the information we gave Zoey as she grew up about Junior, knowing she would be able to find out anything she wanted to find out about him online whenever she decided to look for it. We were intentional in framing him as a troubled person who loved her and that made poor life decisions

"Maybe," I said thoughtfully. "I think we should get another blood test, and we should probably talk to Aideen."

****

Mase offered to come with us for support and to make sure everything added up, but I didn't want to descend on Aideen like the Gestapo.

I decided that I should go alone. I wanted to respect Aideen's privacy because if Junior was Greggins' father, there is no telling what her experience with him had been. Zoey hadn't told anyone except Leese, Mase and me—not even Greg, that she was a match and/or a sibling for him and I applauded her restraint. I had no idea what to expect when I met Aideen, and as I navigated the beauty of the winding, canopied roads, I thought about my time with Junior.

He was handsome and charming, but not the kind that good girls would date. He had a reputation, the kind you get by operating on the wrong side of the law, and he was always around our group even though he was a little older and more of a loner. I was completely infatuated with him and thought the love of a good woman (me) would prompt him to change his ways. We dated for 6 months, and I was blissfully happy, ignoring the warning signs he continued to show me. The chemistry between us was strong and volatile, but I was convinced that my love was all he needed to be the best man he could be, and that's why I overlooked his sporadic demeaning comments and somewhat apathetic attitude.

As soon as we were married and I got pregnant, he was a full-blown controlling alcoholic with no trace of the charming misfit I loved. I felt sorry for that me, so naïve and inexperienced. I used to hear my father's voice saying to me, even though we had no contact once I left home at sixteen, "If you'd shut that damn mouth, he wouldn't have to shut you up." Sometimes I wondered if he was right.

I shook off those memories as I turned into the McGreggor's dirt drive and journeyed through the peach orchard until I was in front of their simple, white clapboard house. I shut off my truck and took a deep breath before exiting, patting their curious Lab, Sport, who had come to greet me, on his bony pointed head.

Aideen opened her screened door and motioned me in.

"No, Sport, you need a bath. Go on and wait for Greg, go on! Excuse him, Lanie, you know he doesn't have any manners."

I smiled. "No worries. I have Mase and he doesn't have any either," I joked.

Her home was just that; homey. It was cozy and decorated in a more sophisticated way than I remembered noticing the last time I was here. I guess I hadn't paid much attention because we had just found out about Greg and his MDS. Not that she couldn't afford nice décor. I knew how much Lisa and I paid her in addition to her regular job, and I knew what she made when she worked for the Downes. She was in demand and as busy as she wanted to be with regards to how much extra work she chose to do. It was then that I realized I didn't really know Aideen. Sure, our children did things together and she had been a fixture, albeit on the fringe, of my life since I arrived in Banjoland, but our conversations were superficial and, sadly, rather meaningless until recently.

I had a feeling that was all going to change in a matter of a few minutes.

"Have a seat," she said, and she set the obligatory glass of sweet tea in front of me as I followed her instructions and got comfortable at her kitchen table. "So what's up?"

She seemed a little nervous and avoided making eye contact with me.

"Aideen," I began, hoping I could say what I wanted to say in a way that she would receive it. "I got some interesting information today and I wanted to talk with you about it." I proceeded to tell her what Z had told me—not knowing what she knew or didn't know—about the blood test results and the implications, and I handed her the lab work.

After she read over it, she set it down gently on the table and offered, "They really do look so much alike."

"So Junior *is* Greg's father?"

"Yes," she said and took a sip of her tea.

Two hours later I had the complete, unedited version of her brief affair with "Johnny", as he was known here. They met when they were both working for the Downes and began what she thought was going to be a relationship, but instead turned out to be "several one-night stands." He told her he was a consultant (I tried not to laugh out loud) and that he was working with the senator on several business opportunities.

Once she got pregnant, he turned into a complete ass, she said, and broke up with her immediately. He never acknowledged her or Greggins, but the senator knew the circumstances and helped her for a while when Greg was a baby. No one else knew and she wanted it kept that way because she was embarrassed that she got caught up in such a situation. She eventually left her job with the Downes to avoid him.

"After Mason shot him and the papers said he was your ex-husband I never really thought about it until I met you, and then, honestly," she said, "I never saw a good reason to bring it up."

I struggled to try and understand her perspective.

"But they've been friends since they were children," I said to her, and she replied that the senator told her it would probably be best not to mention it and I didn't see any reason to disagree. She elaborated that the senator was contributing financially to Greg's expenses. I didn't understand why, and Aideen didn't give any details, so for the moment I thought he was either being a nice guy or more likely, he wanted to have information almost no one else had and for her to be in his debt.

She answered my last question before I asked, and that was why she didn't ask Z to be a donor right from the start once they knew Greggins would need a transfusion. Her reply was simple.

"I know who she is and as soon as I knew she was going to be tested, I knew it would all work out. That's why I have been expecting you," she said.

Chapter 26

"Mom, I'm going to see my bro," Z said, as she headed out the door and over to Aideen's.

She was thrilled with the revelation that Greggins was her brother, and he shared the same feelings, though there was some initial tension between him and Aideen because she withheld this information.

The transfusion had gone well and without complications, and so, with our distraction relegated to the back burner, our focus once again returned to Mase and his upcoming trial. The Grand Jury had indicted, which we expected, and a trial date had been set for early January.

Mase and I were basking in a post love making session when he unexpectedly leaned over and took my face in his hands.

"I love you."

"Me you, too."

"Things might not go our way at trial, and if that's the case, I want you to know that I've made sure you and the kids will be okay."

I didn't know how to respond although this thought had crossed my mind more than once.

"Don't say that," I whispered and kissed him tenderly on the lips.

"I'm serious," he said, pulling back and stroking my hair.

"I know," I said, and he fell asleep holding my hand and leaving me to wonder if I really knew him and what my life would be like this time next year.

****

This was *the* meeting. The one where the investigator was going to discuss whatever information he had gathered to this point and where Mase and AGW were going to go over a mock trial scenario.

It had been difficult for us to gain perspective, as the media circus seemed all encompassing, and it was very challenging to live our lives in total ignorance of cameras outside our home, and pretty much everywhere we went. I tried to be optimistic and rely on the attorneys to find a way out of this unfathomable situation.

The paparazzi had generally left West alone, and Zoey could handle herself. I just had to keep reminding her not to engage with them, as her nature was to tell them off and give them the finger for harassing us.

We arrived at the lawyer's office early, as always, and I could tell Mase was nervous, so I did my best to be supportive and distracting. My attempts at small talk were futile because he was preoccupied with the magnitude of this meeting, so we rode in silence most of the way and remained quiet in the lobby.

Annalise the intern was chipper as usual and went about her routine, offering us drinks and snacks, which we always declined, though I did appreciate her hospitality.

Things were worse than I thought. AGW explained that semen was found on Bella, and this was the first time we'd heard this officially. I mean DNA to me implies semen, so I wasn't surprised, but hearing it officially and then being asked to leave the room so they could have a "private" discussion created the same panic and doubt that day Mase told me he had a son.

"Lanie, I want you to stay, please," and then turning to his attorney he simply said, "my wife will stay."

AGW nodded in deference and began immediately. His words were hard to hear.

"Excuse my candor," he said, "but we need a plausible explanation for why your semen was found on Bella." He looked intently at Mase anticipating some credible reason, just like me.

Before Mase could answer, I interjected with a question of my own.

"Excuse me, but where was the semen—was it on her clothes or on her body?"

Never in my life could I have guessed that those words would come out of my mouth.

Allen Gordon Walker said bluntly, "I had hoped to spare you these details, but the semen was found in and on her vagina, her panties and the bottom of a t-shirt."

My chest tightened and I felt nauseated as I nodded my understanding and sat back in my chair and vacillated between picturing my man having sex with her as she donned panties and a t-shirt (which I took a moment to acknowledge to myself wasn't her style) and visiting him weekly at the state penitentiary.

We waited.

There had been so much interaction between Bella and Mase that I hadn't known about until she died that, understandably I thought, diminished my trust and made me question him. Still, I found it hard to believe he killed her. Worse case in my mind was that they were still having an affair, but I didn't really believe that either. Still, his semen was on, and in, her body and I, like his attorney, was waiting for a plausible explanation.

After reviewing all the evidence that his counselor had organized and placed in a 3-ring binder by date, Mase flung it across the table.

"I thought you had something that could help me," he barked.

"I thought you had something that could help *me*," Walker replied calmly.

Mase stood up, his neck red, his face flushed, and began pacing behind our chairs.

"I didn't have sex with her and I am paying you to prove it!"

All Allen Walker could say was that he needed a believable explanation as to how his semen was on Bella.

"It. Is. Not. Mine." Mase repeated, but the DNA said otherwise.

By the time the meeting was over, Mase was left with a few options: he could take a plea deal if AGW could negotiate one; he could plead guilty—which Mase absolutely refused to consider; or he could allow his team to present a vigorous defense, one that would focus on errors in process, other viable suspects and he would resubmit a DNA sample to exclude possible errors there. Through it all he aggressively maintained his innocence.

****

"Well obviously he's going to fight it," Lisa said as she chased a crawling Clark through my kitchen.

"Yeah, I guess."

"You guess what?" Zoey said, as she tossed her keys into the dish and stuck her head into the opened fridge.

Leese gave her the update.

"Mom," she said in the parental tone she used when she wanted me to understand that I was being

172

unreasonable or ridiculous. "You know he didn't do it, so do what it takes to prove it."

"Easier said than done," I replied, "and Z, you don't know all the details."

She set her cannoli on the counter and reached for her phone that was snugly in her back pocket. She licked some ricotta filling off her lips, texted and swiped twice and handed me her phone. I read the article and handed the phone to Leese.

"Wow," she said, "how do they know all this?"

"Leaks," Z said and finished the last bite of her snack, wiped her hands together and reached for her phone. "So what's your plan—what are we doing to prove he is innocent?"

Chapter 27

The trial was next week, the media was everywhere and Mase still had no explanation of how his semen ended up on, and in Bella. We were barely holding on.

"How can you not know?" I finally blurted out, after spitting toothpaste into the sink. "I thought you ended it with her."

I just couldn't play the supportive wife anymore. Mase was standing at his sink wrapped in a towel, shaving. He rinsed the razor under the hot water.

"Listen," he said dismissively as he patted his face dry. "I just need you to believe me and stop asking me questions I can't answer."

I exploded.

"Oh, okay, because you have such a history of telling the truth," I said sarcastically. "You had so much interaction with her that I didn't know about and now you're telling me not to ask questions about how your semen was *in* her? And to just believe you? You've made me look like an idiot, Mase. Thanks. What a great way to show me how much you love me—you screw her and let me raise her child."

I slammed the bathroom door so hard it sounded like a gunshot.

I was furious, relieved, and sad at the same time.

"Keep an eye on your brothers for me for a while, would you, Z?"

I didn't wait for her response, grabbed my purse, and left, still wearing my pajamas.

****

"Nice ensemble," Lisa said when I barreled through her front door, without knocking (something I usually remember to do since "the kitchen sex incident" a year prior).

I had completely forgotten it was Saturday, our day for group fitness. I sat on her couch and recapped my performance.

"I was wondering when you would have enough," she said.

"Enough what?" Ad asked as he an AJ appeared from the back 40, covered in grass and dirt and rummaged through the fridge for something to drink.

"Enough . . ." and she thought better of what she was going to say while AJ was in the pantry, but her look told Ad all he needed to know.

"Thanks for listening," I said, glancing at my text from Z, "gotta run. Zoey says she has to meet Greggins and RJ."

"RJ?"

"Yes, RJ. I wonder what that's about."

****

The morning before the trial began, we sat together as a family to talk about what might happen.

Mase began, "I just want to say one more time, that I'm sorry this is happening, but West, I hope you know I would never hurt your mom."

"I know, but then why do they think you did?" he said, his eyes glassy and confused.

"Well son," he said, looking him directly, "because they don't have all of the facts."

Clark wobbled over to Zoey, who was sitting on the floor in front of the couch and plopped into her lap.

"I would think the investigators you hired would have come up with something by now," Z said, and took a few minutes to rail about the injustice of this "wrongful prosecution."

"I just want to tell you all that I appreciate your support. I could never do what I'm accused of, but I want you to know that no matter what happens, you will be okay. I've made sure of that."

He then approached each of us and whispered something only that person could hear. When he came to me, he dropped to his knee, held my hand, and whispered softly, "I know this is my fault, and I know you are fed up and don't know what to believe. But I also know that you love me and deep down you know I didn't do this. Thank you for still being here."

He kissed me softly on the cheek, stood and grabbed Clark for Zoey's lap. He walked around the house talking to him while he listened and repeated "love daddy."

"Daddy might be gone for a while," I heard him say, "but when I come home, we will do everything. We will fish and ride the 4-wheeler in the woods, and we will hunt for deer, and I will never leave again, I promise."

I could not hold back the tears, and so I stopped trying.

****

The courthouse was packed with paparazzi, townspeople, friends, acquaintances, and those that just had to see my family unravel in the limited seating that was available. I was surprised, but should not have been, to see the senator and Olivia on the front row of the gallery. It was eerily familiar to the senator's trial, but different, too. This was my husband on trial for killing his child's mother, former lover, lover, and a myriad of other adjectives. The outcome here could change my family forever. Lisa, Ad and I were in the front row opposite the Downes, and Zoey, Greggins and RJ sat directly behind us. West and AJ were at peewee football camp, and I asked the coach to keep an eye on them for obvious reasons, but more in case media showed up. As soon as Mase and his attorneys entered the room, the flashes from the cameras began. Lisa watched the live coverage on her phone with an ear bud in and remarked that it seemed to be fair coverage so far.

The first day dragged on with various motions, but the speculation and commentary from the talking heads was almost too much. They knew Bella was pregnant, and they pondered what my role might be as the jealous wife. In fact, I was served a subpoena to testify that day, but AGW nipped it quickly because, he informed me, a wife cannot be compelled to testify against her husband, and since I wasn't charged, the subpoena was null.

Not surprisingly, the trial didn't take very long, just about a week, because Mase did not have a solid explanation for why his semen was on Bella, and the prosecutor went for that line of questioning almost immediately. I glanced at the coverage Lisa had playing on her phone, and the cameras were focused his parents, who feigned concerned looks and were periodically asked for their thoughts during breaks from the trial.

"I'm just so heartbroken," Olivia said, when asked about Mase's arrest for murdering the pregnant mother of his child, but nevertheless, no matter what, we stand by our son."

The senator added, "We raised him to be responsible

for his choices, and that includes legal consequences of his actions."

I couldn't watch anymore. Mase's attorneys did a very good job, I thought, in creating doubt and offering ideas so that a reasonable doubt about his guilt could be established. Still, when it came down to it, there was no way to account for the semen on Bella. As a last-ditch effort AGW put Mase on the stand. He choked up as he explained that he and Bella were not romantically linked and emphatically insisted he had not had intercourse with her, and I thought he was believable, even though the evidence said otherwise.

The jury was expected to have a verdict tomorrow, Friday, and so we gathered at Lisa's for what felt like a last supper. It was a happy and sad occasion, where friends and supporters came by to share their support and grab a hot-dog and a coke from the grill manned by Ad.

"Don't worry, man," Billy Joe offered, and put his hand on Mase's shoulder. "We'll take care of everything when you're gone."

"I know you will, and I appreciate you, man."

We were all resigned to the fact that Mase was going to be convicted, the verdict seemed to be just a formality.

"Don't worry, honey," Mary Sue said gently, "the truth will eventually come out."

I appreciated her kindness but found myself wondering what the truth was really. If Mase was truly being honest—that he did not have sex with Bella or kill her—then whose baby was it and how did his semen get on her body and her clothes? Did they check the baby's DNA to see if it matched with his? After hearing the evidence, I was convinced pieces to this puzzle were missing and decided to meet with J. Michael Phillips whose services had been very helpful in discovering the circumstances around West's paternity and who Mase had consulted with early on in this case but never had anything substantive to report.

The throng of people who stopped by I think helped Mase realize that despite what the situation looked like, he did have a lot of community support. Part of me was happy about that but the other part was ticked off that they would support him if he had an affair with someone else and a baby on the way and that he could possibly be a murderer. Or maybe they just didn't believe he was guilty. When things wound down and the last group of well-wishers left, I was spent.

"I love you and I'll see you in the morning," Leese said and hugged me hard before they left. Ad and Mase shared a few words and a long, guy hug.

Chapter 28

"Guilty."

The word we dreaded but expected. Lisa's phone showed the running commentary with the heading "*Downes found guilty of murdering pregnant lover. Prosecution will seek death penalty*"

I was flush with emotion and found it hard to breathe.

"Are you okay?" Leese asked, "do you want to go out the back?"

"No," I said, "I just need a minute. I thought I was prepared for this but in this moment my emotions were overwhelming. He was facing the death penalty. I took a few deep breaths while the courtroom buzzed with activity. The senior Downes approached while Mase was taken back to a holding cell and AGW negotiated for bail.

"Lanie, honey," Olivia oozed in her thickest southern drawl, "we are so sorry . . ." Her voice blended with all the others. The senator didn't say a word, but we made eye contact briefly and he had an odd, almost relieved look on his face until he was asked for his opinion on the verdict and stepped right into his song and dance routine about mistakes and consequences. Camera people and reporters were pushing for interviews, and just when I felt like I had pulled it together enough to leave the courtroom, I overheard Zoey speaking with the local Fox reporter. She knew this was against the rules. No one from the family was supposed to engage with them in any way.

"Obviously we believe in his innocence, and we will exhaust all appeal options," she said in a rational, almost business-like manner.

"But Zoey," the reporter countered, "his DNA was on her body. The evidence speaks for itself. How can you possibly believe he is not guilty?"

"It's simple," she said confidently. "When you know him like I know him, then you know he could never commit this crime, which means there is obviously more to the story and that's all I have to say." She took RJ's arm, adjusted her sunglasses, and left the courthouse through the front doors, with Greggins trailing right behind them.

That's my girl. I felt ashamed that I didn't have the confidence in him that she did, but I did not believe for one minute he was a murderer.

****

I met with J. Michael at his office, and he was wearing the same clothes as the first time we met. I think dressing like this, in the cowboy shirt with the snaps, and boots, was a kind of uniform for him. I took a seat at his direction and made pleasantries for a few minutes before cutting to the chase.

"Thanks for meeting with me so quickly," I said. "Things have been crazy, first with the trial and then with the judge denying his bail and while we wait for his sentencing in the next couple of weeks. They are pushing for the death penalty," I whispered, and started to sob. "Walker is trying to . . . get something on the table . . . in exchange for a sentence of life." I thought I should try to get myself under control, but instead I gave in to the tears. J. was a kind gentleman and walked around his mammoth desk and sat in the chair next to me. He scooted it over towards me and held my hand and gave me some tissues. He didn't rush me or offer platitudes or tell me everything was going to be okay. He simply let me have the space I needed to melt down and after several minutes I wiped my tears, blew my nose and took a few deep breaths.

"I'm so sorry. Please forgive me," I offered. "I just wanted to meet with you to make sure that we have done absolutely everything we can, and that we have left no stone unturned. I honestly don't think he killed her."

"I don't think he killed her, either," J agreed. That was nice to hear. "And I have been pursuing an angle that came to light midway through the investigation but that hasn't produced any results so far."

So far?

"What do you mean so far?" I detected the faintest bit of hope surging from underneath a future without Mase.

When he was done explaining I was stunned. I think I was more shocked when he said AGW was aware but didn't share this information with us.

When I asked why we were told any of this, J. Michael explained "there are no definitive answers at the moment, and no one wanted to give either of you false hope."

But this was it. This was the key to Mase's freedom and to the truth. I was sure of it.

Chapter 29

I despised the entire process. I had to request to see Mase, it could only happen during prescribed hours, and I was treated like a criminal just because I wanted to visit with him. He could only have phone calls during a specific window of time and he had to wear that horrible black and white striped suit. I had to be frisked before I could see him and when I did, we were not allowed to touch. It was humiliating for both of us.

Mase had been transferred to the Calhoun Correctional Facility, a state prison about 15 minutes from Clarksville, a few days after the trial while we awaited his sentencing. It was in a scrubby area of Calhoun County and was exactly as I imagined a prison would be, cold, dark, and mean. I had only been able to see him one time for thirty minutes since he was transferred and although he tried hard to be positive, I could tell that reality was sinking in. I hoped this visit would change that. Lisa offered to drive over with me, but I needed her to watch Clark and West, and once I shared J. Michaels information with her, she practically pushed me out the door.

"I can't see him until tomorrow," I reminded her, "and that hurt." I smiled for the first time in a long time.

"This is such great news. I know this is the answer," she said.

"Remember, Leese, don't tell anyone. If J.

Michael's theory is correct, the stuff is going to hit the fan, big time. We can't give anyone the heads up."

"Right," she said. "No worries."

****

I got all the way to the prison to be turned away. All visitation was canceled because a few inmates on Mase's wing got into a brawl. The punishment for everyone was no visitation this week and no phone calls. I was furious at this group punishment mentality, and I hated that Mase was being treated like an inmate. The dehumanization of the people in the prison environment didn't seem fair, whether they were criminals or not.

Life continued and I tried to keep our family in a routine, but Mase was a large presence and it was missed every day. West was involved in school sports along with AJ, and that proved to be a solid distractor. Z, however, had a different distraction.

"What do you think, Mom?"

"I think you have probably already made up your mind."

"Mom."

"I think you can make your own decision in this situation, but if you want my two cents, I say do what you think will make you happy now and *in your future.* You have time."

RJ had proposed getting back together and weathering this distance of her at college and him working for the senator.

"Yeah." She changed the subject. "What's going on with Mase?"

As much as I wanted to tell her everything, I refrained because if this avenue did not pan out, I did not want to be responsible for giving her false hope.

"We've got J. Michael still working on it.

"Well, he hasn't found anything helpful in months, Mom, maybe it's time to get someone high-powered and connected."

She grabbed her keys, picked up Clark who was playing with oversized blocks on his blanket and gave him and loud, wet kiss on his cheek—to which he started giggling and repeating "Zoooeeeyyy."

****

It had been a month and a half since the trial and Mase's sentencing was coming up in the next couple of weeks. We had an appointment with Allen Gordan Walker this week at the prison. He was going to update us on any offers he might have been able to negotiate to keep Mase off death row. I hadn't heard a peep from J. Michael and I was trying not to lose hope.

Mase looked terrible. He had lost weight and his face was gaunt. There was no more façade of hope, but resignation that prison was his life now and in the future, and that could be the best case if he didn't receive the death penalty. I thought it was completely unfair that he was in prison prior to being sentenced, but the court determined he was a flight risk. I brought him some pictures of our family and some approved reading material, but I wasn't allowed to bring him any food or any toiletries—he had to buy all that through the prison system. He dragged the chair out from underneath the bare metal table and reached across to hold my hard.

"No touching," said the guard posted on the inside of the door, watching our every move.

We withdrew our hands from each other at the same time.

"I love you," I said.

"I love you so much," he said, tearing up. "I can't believe this has happened and I know it is all my fault, but Lanie I didn't kill her."

"I know you didn't."

I was about to explain my meeting with J. Michael when the door opened and another guard escorted AGW and J. into the room with us.

"I didn't realize you both were coming today," Mase said.

I didn't realize it either.

They didn't waste any time. Allen Gordon Walker nodded toward J. Michael. "Why don't you tell them what you found?"

"Take a look at this." He handed Mase a manilla folder.

He opened it and read the enclosed document. His eyes got big as he scanned it for a few minutes and then handed it to me.

"Oh my God!" I exclaimed, looking at our counselor for confirmation. "Is this what I think it is?"

"It is," AGW replied

J. Michael explained in detail what he found and how.

"It began with the DNA," he said, "and from there we took the next logical step."

He went on to explain that the DNA evidence found on Bella was semen—something we didn't know originally but found out just before his trial. Conventional serological tests were done implicating Mase, but when J. Michael found out that an actual DNA test had not been done, he had AGW petition the court to submit the semen to the national DNA databases to see if there might be a match. The judge denied the request because he said there was no reason for it but said he could bring it up on his appeal. Mase and I thought that a DNA test was what implicated him, but apparently the process is to use serological tests as they are generally very accurate, unless there is a close relationship between the accused and actual perpetrator. The appeal was filed the day after Mase was convicted and the judge ruled in Mase's favor with regards to submitting the semen at the crime scene to the Combined DNA Index System and the National DNA Index System. Since this was a hail Mary, they didn't mention it because they didn't want to give us false hope.

Because he had offered his DNA during the investigation into Sunglasses' death—"in an effort to find the real murderer and give his family some closure," he had announced, the government had Senator Downes' on file, and the National DNA database showed that his DNA matched what was found on Bella. Sometimes when individuals are close family members, DNA, as opposed to the conventional serological test, is required for definitive conclusions. I had no idea this was the case. But that wasn't the only piece of information J. found. In my opinion, this finding was even better news.

"Once we found out that it wasn't your DNA on Bella," he said, "we took the next logical step—"

"And," interrupted AGW, unable to contain himself, "the baby was the senator's!"

"Oh my God," I said and, feeling immediate relief, reached for Mase's hand.

"No touching!" The guard was still lurking near the door, watching.

"When did this happen and why wasn't I informed?" Mase asked, irritated, but I could also see a lightness come over him.

Solid questions, but I thought he was missing the larger picture and we should focus on expediting his release.

After a thorough discussion covering the timeline, uncertainty of the outcomes of the testing, meeting scheduled for today, etc. Mase seemed satisfied but not pleased with not being made aware of each step as it happened.

"It happened very quickly," J. said, defending their approach. "If I didn't have the connections I do, getting the database results could have taken months. Plus, if testing had led to a dead end, there would be no need to put you on that emotional roller coaster."

Mase expressed again that he didn't like being kept in the dark, and once he made his point, profusely thanked his counsel and his PI.

"So when can I get out of here and when is he going to be arrested?"

"We are working on it as we speak," Walker said. "Have to meet with the prosecutors, petition for your conviction to be overturned or at the minimum a new trial."

Although we were frustrated his release was not immediate, we now saw a light at the end of the tunnel. Mase was emboldened to give me a quick kiss as he was escorted from our meeting room back to his cell and winked as he left my sight.

****

It had taken six excruciating weeks for Mase to be released. AGW said the police wanted to have the senator in custody first and that they had to have a long meeting with prosecutors to show them the DNA results—to see if they wanted to prosecute him— and to make a direct appeal to the court to have Mase's conviction overturned.

On the ride home from prison we were exuberant. Our first stop was a Checker's drive-in so he could get three chili cheese dogs. We chatted and joked and were so filled with relief and hope that we swore not to take any day, even the worst, for granted.

"I'm sorry I ever had a doubt about your innocence," I said, softly and sincerely, my hand resting on his lap while he drove.

"I don't blame you, Lane. I gave you reason to doubt me. I'll do my best to never do that again."

He pulled off the highway onto an isolated dirt road and swallowed the last bite of his chili dog. He wiped his mouth on a crumpled napkin and then pulled me across the seat onto his lap.

He kissed me hard and long and with passion and need. I missed him so much. His smell, the feel of his body, the way he touched me. His whole being. I felt like he was consuming me and his arousal was evident with me on his lap.

"I need you," he whispered and reached under my t-shirt to unhook my bra.

"Here?" I asked, but I couldn't help myself. I was overwhelmed with desire for him.

"Yes, here."

He lifted my shirt over my head exposing my breasts, while I massaged the bulge in his pants.

"The shifter is in my back," I panted, and he opened his door and turned so one leg was on the ground the other was in the floorboard. I sat on his lap facing him, slipped off my shorts and panties while he exposed himself. I slid on top of him in a grinding motion until we climaxed intensely. It was one of the most intimate experiences I ever had.

We dressed quickly and headed to the house, where everyone was waiting.

"Daddy's home!" Mase bellowed as he rounded the front of the car to open my door.

West ran to him and jumped into his arms.

"I love you, Dad!"

"You've grown two feet!" Mase set him gently on the ground.

Clark toddled over and Mase scooped him up and smothered him with kisses.

"How's my big boy?"

"Daddy home. Daddy home," he jabbered.

We walked towards the porch where Z, RJ and Greggins were waiting. Z met him at the top of the stairs with a cold beer and had a flute of champagne for me.

"I told them all along you were innocent." She hugged him hard. "I'm glad you're home."

"I know you did," Mase responded, "and I can't tell you how much your loyalty means to me." He choked up a little.

"And, gentlemen, I see that the gang is together again."

They shook hands, hugged and did the back-slap thing the way men do.

"Home sweet home," Mase said and sat on the swing with his feet in my lap. And we took a collective breath.

Chapter 30

Chaos reigned once again. I was so sick of trials and drama and media. But Mase and I were both on the same page with our opinion of this one and that is we would have a front row seat to watch the conviction of a man who was going to let his son get the death penalty for a crime that he did not commit. This trial was far more publicized than his last, which I didn't think was possible. In addition to the familiar news trucks and the ever-present media faces, the tabloids had descended upon us like vultures searching for one salacious tidbit that they could turn into a front page, "new angle" story. It was on all of the national news morning shows. It was literally everywhere. Mase and I had to have a meeting with our closest friends after Billy Joe, in an attempt to normalize our family to the reporter, mentioned a harmless gathering that included a hog hunt, which was immediately interpreted and presented as a modern-day Deliverance story. The tabloid presented us as hillbillies to intrigue their readers, despite the fact that we had other, more sophisticated aspects to our lives as well.

The other glaring difference between this trial and his last, was the senator seemed genuinely worried. He was no longer the cocky, arrogant bureaucrat despite his efforts to appear that way.

"Don't you think it's odd that your mom is standing by him?" I asked Mase not long after the trial had begun.

"Don't be fooled," he replied. "Just because she appears in public with him doesn't mean she's all in."

I thought about this for a moment and realized I should have known better. In all the years I had known Olivia, she never showed her hand, not once. It made me wonder what she was thinking and what her plans were.

****

The courtroom was packed when the jury returned with their verdict. Thankfully, cameras and news people were banished to the periphery of the outside lobby, so we didn't have to worry that our every facial expression was going to be broadcast for the world to see like it was during Mase's trial. At least they learned something about media management in the courtroom. We were front row ready, with Ad and Leese and Z and RJ, who looked like they were on the verge of reuniting. I was surprised at what a strong defense the senator's attorneys had been able to present, given the DNA evidence and that Bella was pregnant with his child. They did their best to create doubt surrounding the evidence gathering process and the subsequent conclusions drawn by the investigative team. I honestly went from having no doubt whatsoever about his guilt, to wondering if the jury—just one member—would follow the defense team's logic. The defense attorneys did their best to paint Mase as someone who could have plausibly committed the murder, after all, he did have an affair with her while he was married and how did we really know it was over? And while that bothered me a lot, in the big scheme of life we were all grateful that his conviction was overturned, so everything else that happened seemed secondary.

"Mr. Foreman," the judge queried, "have you

reached a verdict?"

"We have, your honor."

The bailiff took the crumpled paper from the foreman's hand and gave it carefully to the judge.

"What say you?"

The silence was thick with anticipation. Mase's sweaty fingers were intertwined with mine, and Lisa's hand rested gently on my arm.

"We the jury, find the defendant, Mason W. Downes, III. . . guilty of 1st degree murder as charged."

Pandemonium erupted before the man could finish speaking. Senator Downes sat in his chair at the defense table and appeared bewildered and lost. Anyone else might have felt sorry for him. The judge tried to regain order, but it wasn't happening. We decided before we arrived at the courthouse that we would exit through the service entrance in the back to avoid the onslaught of media and tabloid attention we were likely to receive no matter what the jury decided. This exit was different than the regular back door exits in that it was on the side of the building and so nondescript that it looked like a window. If you didn't spend much time at the courthouse, you would never notice it. Upon Mase's cue, we all filed as discreetly as possible one at a time out of the courtroom and through the hallway next to the judge's chambers, where no media were allowed. We followed one after another through the emergency exit door and down the stairs until we emerged in a dusty, gray, cement hallway. Surprisingly, someone was already there.

"Mother?" Mase said.

"Son," she replied while he kissed her on the cheek. "Everyone," she acknowledged.

"I see you have the same plan we do," Mase commented.

I hadn't noticed her leaving the courtroom. She nodded in response and without further conversation slipped out the door and discreetly into the nondescript sedan that pulled up to aid in her escape. We followed shortly after and disappeared amid the reporters clamoring for comment from anyone who would offer.

Chapter 31

The appeal process didn't take as long as we thought it might, and somehow, he was allowed to do interviews from prison, several times, where he proclaimed his innocence and promoted an image of a misunderstood victim. It didn't stop there. He hired the best legal team money could buy, and they organized interview after interview with expert after expert to poke holes in the case against, and ultimately, I think, to sway public opinion.

"He's pretty convincing," I mentioned after a particularly emotional interview we saw on Fox.

"You would be too if your life depended on it," Mase replied.

What was unusual to me, though at this point I'm not sure why, was Olivia's behavior. She appeared in public by his side, though she never spoke on camera. Otherwise, she went about her life, playing tennis and lunching at the Club. It was like she was two completely different people.

In the end, the publicity tour was unsuccessful and Senator Downes' conviction was upheld, as was his life sentence—his high-powered team was able to keep him off death row. It didn't make me as happy as I thought it would, and Mase didn't say much about it except that he got what he deserved.

We were coming to terms with everything that

happened in the past year, not only the bad, but we also now had two sons, and Zoey had two half-brothers to go along with her step- brother.

"You should put this in your book," Leese kept telling me. "Your whole life is a book!"

"I might. I just might. If it doesn't give me PTSD."

She laughed.

Our joviality was interrupted when Mase got a text.

"It's from Mother," he offered. "She's out of the country."

"Andorra?" Leese and I said in unison, joking. She spent so much time in this small country south of France we thought one day she would finally move there.

"Yes, actually." He read the rest of the text silently. After a minute he handed me the phone.

Leese peered over my shoulder. "Well, damn," she said.

The text was an explanation. It explained that when Olivia discovered Bella was pregnant with the senator's child, through an unfortunate misstep by Bella's physician's office, that was the last straw. She'd finally had enough.

Good for her, I thought as I continued to read. It was the next sentence that changed everything.

"That's why I killed her."

Her very last sentence was simple and devoid of emotion, "Andorra does not have an extradition treaty with the United States, so I will be enjoying life here— please delete this message once you've read it." And after he read it a few more times, that is exactly what he did.

A word about the author...

Kim has always been a storyteller, and after moving South and raising her children, she took advantage of the fertile opportunities surrounding her life in the Deep South to pen her first full-length novel. The contrast in lifestyle from her childhood in upstate New York to that of rural Southern life afforded her many opportunities to broaden her perspective on the different meanings of American life. She currently works in the "City" and returns every evening to life on her farm with her husband and mandatory dog.

Thank you for purchasing
this publication of The Wild Rose Press, Inc.

For questions or more information
contact us at
info@thewildrosepress.com.

The Wild Rose Press, Inc.
www.thewildrosepress.com

www.ingramcontent.com/pod-product-compliance
Lightning Source LLC
Chambersburg PA
CBHW070504260626
47161CB00004B/1454